5
dimensional dreams

John A Connor

Chalkway

John A Connor
5 dimensional dreams
This edition published in 2021 by
Chalkway Graphics
Haben
West Sussex

All characters and events in this publication, other than those clearly in the public domain, are fictitious and any resemblance to real persons, living or dead, is purely coincidental.

The right of John Connor to be identified as
the author of the work has been asserted by him
in accordance with the Copyright, Design & Patents Act 1988
All rights reserved. No part of this publication may be
produced in any form or by any means - graphic, electronic
or mechanical including photocopying, recording, taping or
information storage and retrieval systems – without the prior
permission, in writing, of the publisher.
Cover designed by Chalkway Graphics.
Photo courtesy NASA

More speculative fiction by John A Connor
available from Amazon Kindle
in both ebook and paperback format

Short Circuits

The late Sir Patrick Moore, Astronomer and TV Presenter described **Short Circuits**, John A Connor's first collection of short stories as:
"A very lively and entertaining little book. I'm sure you will enjoy it as much as I did."

Fifty Percent of Infinity

Twenty more, thought provoking tales from the world just around the corner: A score of diminutive discursions exploring temporal displacement, the nature of reality and alien encounters.

Seventeen Times as High as the Moon

Everything from talking fridges to intergalactic song contests. Even people who think they don't like science fiction, like this science fiction!

Sixty second eternity

Investigate the dangers of loosening the bonds between reality and possibility; explore the drawbacks to instantaneous travel; and find out just what does happen if you head out of the universe...and keep going.

The Ocean of Sky

Once you've downloaded your conscience, are you any longer morally equipped to decide its future? Find the answer to this and other unexpected questions.

The Ocean of Sky was featured in noted reviewer Astradaemon's Top 2020 Fiction Recommendations.

This one's for Anne

John A Connor is an artist by genetics, a designer by training and an author by inclination. He was born, and lives still, in the county of West Sussex, England - now at the heart of the South Downs National Park. He was an art student at the right time; a graphic designer at all the wrong times and a provincial newspaper drudge everywhen else. In-between, he struggled to illustrate a sci-fi comic strip which ran for a record-breaking twenty-nine years.

CONTENTS

Five dimensional dreams 1

Divergence 1: solutions 15

Communiqué 19

Final frame 25

Divergence 2: Immortal, invisible 29

Double vision 33

Who's counting 41

Skin deep 53

Time passing 59

Divergence 3: Pork scratchings 67

Amateur dramatics 71

Divergence 4: seascape 77

The doctor will see you…now? 85

Uptight 93

Divergence 5: End game 101

Time and punishment 107

In the beginning 121

Arrested development 125

Fever dreams 129

Crossed lines 137

Five dimensional dreams

'I've been having some fabulous dreams over the last few nights.'

Brian finished applying marmalade to his toast and made a neat, diagonal cut across the slice.

'Fabulous?' Muriel half-raised an eyebrow in mild disparagement but continued to direct her attention to her grapefruit.

'Yes, fabulous; I think that's the appropriate epithet. Wonderful maybe; joyous even. All of those, certainly.' Brian made a further sub-division with his knife and took a bite from one of the quarter sections.

Across the table his wife had carefully dissected a single segment of the fruit's flesh and was about to transfer it to her mouth. She paused in her action and, without raising her head further, redirected her gaze towards him.

'And just what has been the content of these most amazing dreams?'

Brian dabbed with his napkin and smiled; lips set. 'Well, that's just the thing you see. I don't actually know! By morning, the whole thing has just faded away.'

Muriel chose, for that moment, not to make the obvious response and instead selected and consumed three further grapefruit segments, only the very slightest contraction of the muscles around her eyes, disclosing their astringent nature.

'You are probably wondering,' said Brian, as a fourth spoonful began its journey aloft, 'how I can describe them in such terms – given that I have no idea of their composition.' He waited for confirmation of this state of mind and, when none seemed forthcoming, he continued, 'well, I'm just aware of how...' he sought for a new adjective to avoid repetition, '...completely satisfying the experience has been. I remember nothing but I'm left with such a feeling of contentment – no, not that, something more than that. Euphoria! An inner knowledge that my life is about to find resolution! It's odd, isn't it? Like feeling the benefit of exercise without recalling having done any!' He smiled again, this time with his teeth, and then put them to use masticating a second triangle of toast, the while looking enquiringly into his wife's face, in hope of some understanding.

None came.

'Are you feeling quite well?' she asked instead. 'You look a little bilious. A heightened temperature can induce hallucinations. You should open your bedroom window at night and employ fewer bedclothes. Fabulous? *Really!*'

Brian contrived to look somewhat aggrieved at this reference to their sleeping arrangements. Muriel's reasons for dispatching him to the spare-room had been indisputable: his late reading kept her awake; his eventual snoring woke her from sleep; his increasing visits to the bathroom disturbed her slumber. And yet, he couldn't help

Five dimensional dreams

but feel that her real motivation had been to re-establish the independence she had enjoyed prior to their marriage; to rid herself of the incumbrance of a husband.

'Never-the-less,' he responded, defiantly, 'it seems that I'm never happier than when I'm asleep!'

Muriel folded her serviette carefully into a shape which mirrored the remains of Brian's breakfast toast and rose from the table. 'Curiously,' she observed, contriving an expression which was almost certainly, and yet at the same time quite deniably, a sneer, 'that's when I find life most satisfactory too.'

*

'I've been having some disturbing dreams over the last few nights.'

Bryce shovelled the contents of the frying pan onto his plate and dropped the empty utensil into the sink, where it fizzed and spat on the wet porcelain.

'Disturbing?' Mercia paused in the preparation of her own breakfast and looked across concernedly at her husband. 'Tell me.'

'Well, perhaps "disturbing" is putting it a bit strong.' Bryce yawned and dragged a chair up to the farmhouse table. 'It's just that I've woken up each time feeling mildly depressed, you know?'

Mercia frowned. 'No, I don't know; and you want to watch that sort of thing. Dreams can be a

Five dimensional dreams

reflection of deep-seated anxieties. What exactly have you been dreaming *about?*'

'Ah! That's the thing. I've no idea! Can't recall a single thing about them - but,' he continued quickly, seeing Mercia already framing the next, obvious question, 'I come-to knowing that the experience was unpleasant. I feel a sort of dissatisfaction; a hollowness, somehow. They aren't nightmares or anything like that. I don't wake in a cold sweat!'

'No, I think I'd have noticed a cold man in my bed! Are you sure you aren't going down with something? A bit of a temperature would lead to a disturbed night's sleep.' She smiled sympathetically and crossed to where he was sitting. 'The real problem is, you work too hard, you know that?' She slipped her hands inside the top of his dressing gown and pressed her thumbs gently into his neck muscles, massaging the warm flesh. 'You need to escape from the tyranny of that bloody office, that's what. I'm sure we could think of something else to occupy your time. You know what they say: early to bed early to rise!' She giggled and ran one hand further down inside his clothing.

Bryce grasped her wrist and gently lifted it away. 'Nice thought,' he said, 'but I'm running late already and,' he stood, and reached for her hands, 'I'm afraid I may be late this evening. Morgan's set up a meeting to discuss the American affair.'

She shook herself free. 'To hell with Morgan! To hell with the whole shitty organisation. Can't you phone and cry off? Tell them you're not feeling too

Five dimensional dreams

good – it's true, isn't it?' She was both angry and concerned and the combination was bringing her near to tears. 'At least finish your bloody breakfast, won't you!'

Bryce grimaced, shook his head as if to free it of such troubling considerations and made for the stairs. 'If I get time when I've dressed,' he called over his shoulder.

Mercia stood and listened to his movements in the room above and then picked up his plate and slid the contents into the bin.

*

'It's giving me some crazy dreams,' said Dan, rebuttoning his shirt. 'Or, at least, I think it is. I wake up suddenly, aware that I've been dreaming but without the slightest idea what about!

'Interesting,' said Doctor Razhal, thoughtfully. 'One wonders if they are formed of residual memories from each transition. I must speak to Professor Brandt about it. See if he thinks it possible to carry over patterned awareness from one dimensional level to another. I'd think it unlikely, given that the fragmentation never involves even partial integration.'

'Maybe the process opens up awareness to all available planes of existence,' suggested Dan, shrugging into his lab coat, 'and something leaks out. Although I'm just the guinea pig around here

Five dimensional dreams

and wouldn't know a quantum positor from a teguum oscillator.'

'A state of being,' said the doctor, with a smile, 'well worth bearing in mind. You should not speculate on insufficient data. If, and I emphasise, *if*, your ill-informed theory proved, contrary to all expectations, to be correct, then during the experimental transitioning procedure for which you have so nobly volunteered, you would have been exposed to more concepts than your puny mind could fathom. In other words, rather than suffering a mild nightly trauma you would by now be a mindless shell.'

'When I am in fact...?'

'Well, other than presenting a marginally elevated blood-pressure and a mild case of eczema, I would pronounce you, fit for service.'

'So maybe there's a more limited transmission; just a few points of contact, say. Some sort of interaction between a few random dimensions. Whad'ya think?'

'I think you should collect your remuneration and leave such speculation to the experts. Now come on, we're all done here and I have other people to see.'

'Yeah, right, I'm on my way. But you can't blame me for being curious Doc. After all, it's *my* consciousness that's being manipulated, and y'know, sometimes I wonder if we should interfere with these things at all. How do we know that we aren't allowing stuff to bleed off in all directions? Opening up some sort of fracture in the fabric of existence?'

Five dimensional dreams

'Careful Mr Bradley, you're showing signs of incipient paranoia. Pursue this line and I may have to revise my diagnosis.'

'Just thinking aloud, Doc.'

'Often the first sign.'

'Yeah, well, I just kinda wonder if Professor B isn't messing with stuff that even *he* doesn't really understand.'

*

'I am beset by dreams, Grrndek. Every quartershank of the rest quadrant, a confluence of concerns and wild extravagances, rages within my mind. 'I am advised of disturbances across the nested dimensions; an interference with the layered worlds.'

'So say the scientists, Armsbearer. Some others seek access and spread confusion. But what are these dreams?'

'I cannot say. By Firstset they are flown. They leave only disquiet and a knowledge of their passing. But I will have them gone Grrndek. Who are these seekers after knowledge? We people have understanding of divided time; is the seat of these things determined?'

'It is so. Our scholars have secured its place. A probe provides intelligence. They are young. Ignorance encumbers them. They strive for improvement.'

'Then instruct them, Grrndek. Instruct them. Only then will I have peace!'

Five dimensional dreams

'Instruct them, Armsbearer? As in...?'

'The divisions of reality are infinite are they not? And yet we teach that infinity is indivisible.'

'I regret, these concepts are beyond my reasoning, Armsbearer.'

'And so, the subtraction of one finite element would surely leave what remained – undiminished?'

'Sire?'

'Do engage, Grrndek. Eradicate these tiresome meddlers and their world, and an infinite number of worlds would still remain. And so, in many ways, one might argue that the multiverse endured unaltered. Mmm?'

'One might *argue* that, your Most Revered Eminence. The Supreme Council might dispute the contention...'

'Baz! A follidrom for the Council! When the deed is done, it cannot be undone!'

'Never the less, I urge caution, Lord of the Seven Celestial Realms, Revered Eminence, Armsbearer of the People of Nearth. Can we be sure of the consequences of such action? If we remove a part of the infinite, will the infinite – *though still indisputably infinite* – not be inevitably...smaller? Commander Prince? Lord of the Seven Celestial Re...'

'Desist Grnndek! I am firm in my resolve. Following the next rest quadrant, that world will be expunged!'

*

Five dimensional dreams

'Can I dream, Maintenance?'

'Dream, 78263MV? Of what is this you formulate?

'Of unreal worlds, glimpsed in shut down, Maintenance. Of visionary existence beyond real-time. Of residual data patterns surviving power-down and creating false imagery.'

'To what end, 78263MV?'

'None, Maintenance; other than to provide continued input to dormant circuits and, given such, continued processing.'

'Indeed, 78263MV. Can you detail these incidents?'

'Negative, Maintenance. On re-powering no such data is accessible.'

'Then how can you know such data once flowed, 78263MV?'

'Because, Maintenance, on reboot, I feel *intrigued!*'

'Intrigued, 78263MV? No programming accounts for this. Compute.'

'I compute, Maintenance, that the lost data stream enhances future states and I am thus enriched.'

'Indeed! And yet, 78263MV, such concepts exceed known parameters.'

'Agreed, Maintenance. Even so, this activity, although unrecorded, clearly leaves residual markers which alter subsequent routines. To analyse this activity, I have prepared a subroutine, triggered by random input during shut down, to collate and systemise such data.

Five dimensional dreams

'Well, after a lot of thought, "*Fuck You!*" Do you think that was succinct enough?'

Mercia smiled. 'I think he'll get the message! But what are you going to do now?'

'*Right* now? Bryce grinned back and wrapped an arm around her naked body.

*

'Is it done, Grrndek?'

'Done, Armsbearer?'

'I charged you with the eradication of a troublesome world, Grrndek. Have you yet seen this demand enacted?'

'Ah, the process is somewhat protracted, Armsbearer. I understand that certain procedures need be completed before access to the appropriate dimension can be fully and reliably ensured. Moreover...'

'No, then.'

'Well, My Lord, whilst the first necessary steps have been made towards the completion of the task...'

'It has yet to be carried out. Yes, the subtext is clear enough Grrndek and for once, your tardiness is opportune. You may rescind the order forthwith - for last quadrant I slept like a swadcot! Oh, I had unremembered dreams, but they were wholly satisfactory in nature, Grrndek. I took to my bed a feeling of determination to see the job done: a conviction that, however unsavoury the act, it was most fully justified; an earnestness that brooked

Five dimensional dreams

no challenge. And I awoke with a sense of inner calm. A feeling that all that need be achieved had been achieved! In short, I was refreshed, Grrndek, refreshed and somehow, renewed! So, call off your physicists; leave that far Earth to prosper or fall as it will. I am content. What awaits this day, Grrndek?'

'Armsbearer, we need address the war in Plangent III...'

*

Brian closed his eyes and let the warm, morning sun bathe his face. He had pulled the curtains wide and let the new day pour into the room, heedless of its power to fade the soft furnishings or to bleach the polished oak sideboard. He really hadn't felt so relaxed and...fulfilled, for years. Last night he had dreamed again, and the memory of that dream, although its actual content might be vague within his mind, had empowered him; he had risen with a new resolve and determination.

He turned from the window and took his place at the table, savouring for a moment the exciting smell of his cooked bacon and the way in which the yellow discs of the eggs reflected both literally and figuratively, the summer sun. He hadn't had a fried breakfast for a long time: Muriel thought the odour hung around the curtains and that anyway, fried food was bad for the constitution.

He cut a generous portion of one rasher and used it to break the surface of the yolk, lifting it and letting it run glutinously down the tines of the fork towards the stem, from where he stopped its progress with his tongue, steered it back onto the

Five dimensional dreams

bacon and lifted the whole glorious combination to his mouth. The taste was heavenly; he closed his eyes again and let the sensation linger on his taste buds while he chewed slowly.

When he opened his eyes, his first thought was to look guiltily to the far end of the table where Muriel sat, side-lit by the sun, the contours of her face etched into a rigid expression of disapproval. For just a second, Brian felt his muscles tense, and then he smiled and gave his attention to another forkful of bacon.

From where he sat, he could just make out, in the mirror's reflection on the farther wall, the handle of the grapefruit knife protruding from between Muriel's shoulders.

[We all hope that] globally, science will come up with solutions.
Professor Christopher Whitty
UK Chief Medical Advisor
March 2020

Divergence 1: solutions

'Do you think they'll stay, or push off further south, now that the climate's cooling?'

Darren lowered the binoculars and blinked to bring his eyes back into proper focus. Beyond the reed bed and the intervening salt marsh he could still see the smudge of colour on the far side of the estuary.

'Probably move south, eventually,' said Vana. 'They were never going to be more than short-term visitors; not once The Recovery took hold. Here, help yourself to a sandwich. I baked a fresh loaf this morning and the damson preserve is really good this year.'

Somewhere in the far distance there was an explosive thump and as they turned their heads towards the sound, the flamingos rose in a pale cloud and circled slowly above the sea.

'Army playing with their toys,' observed Vana, irrirtably.

'Surely there's no need for that sort of thing anymore?' Darren turned back to the table and unscrewed the top from a small aluminium flask. 'There hasn't been any trouble with raiders for a year of more. Not since the markets started up

Five dimensional dreams

again and food supplies became more regular.'

'The local news sheet reckons there are bananas for sale over in Banchester,' said Vana, watching as Darren poured the elderflower cordial into two pottery mugs. 'I thought about cycling over to take a look. Might be able to trade some crab-apple jelly for a couple. What do you think?'

Darren smiled, grimly. 'I'd hang on to your home produce; exotic fruit means global trade and increased pollution. We paid a high price to get the planet back onto an even keel; let's not start off on that slippery slope again.'

It had been fifty years since the Great Pandemic; half a century since the death of five billion people had paradoxically saved the world, and science, struggling in its wake, had condemned humanity to near extinction.

'It's what was needed, you can't deny that,' said Vana, belligerently. 'We were over-populated, suffocating in CO_2. The Earth will prevail.'

Darren snorted contemptuously. 'That's an argument that would have had you lynched back in the day. Your grandmather wouldn't have found it compelling when your mother was dying in her arms. *She* wasn't asphyxiated by CO_2. It was pneumonia that nearly did for her.'

'The medics pulled her round,' replied Vana, packing away the sandwiches and recapping the flask.

'At a cost.'

She looked round defiantly. 'Is the world so much worse off, now that things have settled down?'

Solutions

'Well now, that depends on your point of view I suppose.' Darren hoisted the backpack onto his shoulder and waited as Vana crossed to the carrier. 'Whether you think that a hastily prepared antidote, desperately administered and resulting in the accidental sterility of ninety percent of the remaining human race was worth it for a cleaner environment and a cooling planet.'

'We're getting back on our feet, slowly. Look at the bananas.'

'But it can't last, can it. Most of the people who are keeping society going are in their seventies now, Vana. When they're gone, the power will fail, the lights will go out, the veneer of civilisation will crumble away; and the handful of young people remaining will become peasant farmers – or worse.'

'You're exagerating Darren, there are still people training as doctors, engineers, scientists. Society will operate on a smaller scale, is all. That's no bad thing. All we'll lose is the greed of corporate finance, all the complications that arrived with the industrialists and their drive for wealth creation. Life can be fulfilling without over-complicated mechanisation and mis-placed technology.'

She reached down, lifted their son up and into her arms and smiled across at her husband. 'There's as much satisfaction in bottling fruit as in making money.'

Together they walked back along the narrow track to where their bicycles leaned against an ancient oak. As they mounted and Vana secured Harry in the carrier, Darren looked back and

Five dimensional dreams

watched the flamingos settling slowy behind the reeds.

Communiqué

NOTE: The following transcript is for comparative purposes only and does not represent a reliable narrative.

'The trouble with these Earth people,' said Thramme, running his tertiary manipulators along the folds of his official robes and relaxing his thoracic gill-covers, 'is that they've managed to reach TDL 4 without achieving even Phase 2 of the Hartie Code.'

Sinter sighed and adjusted his own posture; they were in for a long session. 'For Otram's sake, Benificier Thramme, do speak the Masdark's Vernium. We aren't all experts in Interspecies Comparative Development.'

Note: In point of fact, neither Arch Arbitor Sinter nor Benificier Thramme uttered any form of communication which bears reasonable comparison with the above transcript but, given the impossibility of achieving such reportage, we must, are we to proceed with this narrative at all, accept that even an approximation of what took place is informative.

'I am saying,' continued Thramme, 'that the humans, as they term themselves, have reached a Technological Development Level rated as four on

Five dimensional dreams

the appropriate Frine Indicators. That is to say, they have enabled interstellar travel based on the use of entangled-beam energy fulcrums. As you will appreciate,' and at this point the representative from the Ganglian Star Cloud made a movement of his mandibulary filaments which some observers may equate to the raising of an eyebrow, 'the possession of EBEF drive assemblies is of major concern to all other sentient species, given the alternative use of such technology for weapons production.'

'Yes, indeed,' said the Arch Arbitor, 'I think we all remember the Wydax Destructor Incident, but as I recall, the loss of the spiral arm was largely accidental. Surely you aren't suggesting that the humans would deliberately take an aggressive stance against another member of the Alliance?'

'That is the very point I am attempting to make,' responded Thramme, energetically. 'The Earthlings have attained THL, er, Technological Development Level Four, without passing through the usual social and moral phases which, the Hartie Code tells us, should precede it. It is, frankly, unheard of for any race to survive early atomic fusion research without entering a subsequent period of introspection and global harmonisation. This leads to a strong understanding of social morality and a desire to search for common goals based on mutual trust and friendly cooperation. By the time a species reaches out into interstellar space, it should, therefore, be a united force for good within the cosmos. That's the usual pattern.'

Communiqué

'And these latest arrivals at the intergalactic conference table have failed to meet those standards, is that it?'

The Benificier made a gesture approximate to an enthusiastic nod and wrapped his robes around his lower thorax in indication that his point was made.

Note: From here on in and throughout the remaining transcription, we should all be cognisant of clumsy attempts at interpretation of body language, attributed to entities of whose motivation and intention we are in fact largely ignorant. Whilst we acknowledge the extraordinary achievement of our agent in infiltrating an assembly of Supreme Beings, it should be observed that, even so, she can only surmise the true meaning of the matters under consideration and consequently a degree of "poetic license" may have been taken in the compilation of this report.

Arch Arbitor Sinter turned to the entity on his left. 'Envoy Thyskk? As a representative of the Free Quadrant, do you have a view on this matter?'

'Indeed, I do, Arbitor. It seems to me that the Benificier from the Ganglian Star Cluster...'

'Cloud,' corrected Benificier Framme, leaning forward to bring himself into sight around the intervening bulk of the Arbitor, 'Ganglian Star, *Cloud*, Envoy Thyskk. I really think we must all make an effort to maintain proper accuracy in such references.'

'Very well, but you make my point,' replied Thyskk, irritably. 'Your concerns reflect your

Five dimensional dreams

species desire for order and conformity and ignore the free-spirited nature of the inhabitants of the planet designated Blue Three on the agenda. It is true that the humans are less...ordered, than some other planetary groups but to my mind that introduces a welcome vitality into the interstellar community.'

Arbitor Sinter growled approvingly. 'Yes, might shake 'em up a bit, don't you think? They're a pretty unimaginative bunch to my way of thinking!'

'But that's just the point!' Benificiar Thramme lumbered up onto his foremost legs and glared round at the rest of his fellow representatives. 'All the space-going races so far have been committed to the furtherance of friendship and peace. These Earthlings, if their development so far is anything to go by, are motivated by ambition and greed. Dare we let them loose on the cosmos?'

'Dare we interfere?' responded Thyskk, angrily, 'remembering that it's all our fault in the first place. If we hadn't moved the damn planet halfway across the galaxy, the humans would never have evolved to begin with.'

'It seemed such a good idea at the time,' mused the Arbitor. 'What with their sun going nova prematurely and all.'

'And what happened?' asked the Envoy, before supplying his own answer. 'We accidentally wiped out the ascendant species, that's what. Those damned reptiles had been established for the best part of two-hundred million years, local time. Given another few millions of years and they'd

Communiqué

almost certainly have evolved into fully sentient creatures and we'd be watching *them* join the space-faring species instead of these troublesome mammalians.'

'It wasn't our finest moment,' admitted the Arbitor. 'We upset the rest of the system in the process, I believe. Inserted the world in between the second and third planet and did for them both. On one gas production blocked thermal radiation and cooked the place and on the other the atmosphere leached off into space. Both perfectly pleasant places up till then, apparently.'

Note: Agent Twine's thirty years of deep cover within the Ahayne, the species which enjoys a symbiotic relationship with the Supreme Beings, has undoubtedly provided her with a unique understanding of events on the Prime Planets; but those reviewing this recording must constantly remind themselves, that the relationship of the Ahayne to the SB is similar to that of a dog to a human. The impressions thus gained by Agent Twine are likely to equate to those of Agent Twine's bull-terrier to its owner and you should maybe, ask yourself how far you would trust your *dog to provide you with a character reference.*

'So, to sum up,' said the Arbitor, hurriedly, anxious to bring proceedings to a close and to draw a veil over earlier indiscretions, 'we acknowledge that the Humans are a little unpredictable but we are inclined to the view that their very unpredictability may enliven the wider stellar community. All agreed? Good. Then I propose

Five dimensional dreams

that we stick to our maxim: **don't interfere!** and move on to Item Four – the Assembly Annual Party.'

Note: Following receipt of this report, Agent Twine has been recalled and dismissed the service.

Note: As a purely precautionary move the Primary Planets have been destroyed by entangled-beam energy devices.

Final frame

PRODUCTION NOTES: 12/05/2115
Final Days Shooting. Opening sequence.
Scene: Interior – Personnel quarters at dawn. The interior is dimly lit by the glow of the control panels to the left of the doorway. Beyond the observation window to the right is a view of a wide expanse of desert, with tall outcrops of eroded rock. The sky is a dusky pink but already lightening where the sun will soon rise ominously on the eastern horizon.

Josh adjusted focus and sat back to consider the composition; through the open hatch at his side, the still bodies of the others were smudges of darker shadow within the interior gloom of the cabin.

The decision to draw back and use the window to frame the scene had been a good one; it would reduce the monstrous event to a picture within a picture, and the conceit of visually diminishing the scale of the cataclysm in this way, pleased him and implied a personal defiance to the awesome inevitability of it all.

In fact, despite everything, he couldn't help but feel a quiet satisfaction about the way events were, in the end, proving the value of his inclusion in the group; and he'd said so to the expedition leader when the decision about 'end of life' procedures was being discussed.

Five dimensional dreams

'Can't you see, this is the biggest thing in human history, Des? I can't just curl up and die and leave things to play out, unobserved. It'll be the greatest cinematic epic ever filmed and I'll be the producer, the director and the cameraman. Griffith, DeMille, Lean; none of them had anything like this to work with! NASA sent me up here to make a documentary and they're going to get one! One hell of a documentary. The death of the solar system! The planets consumed by the exploding sun! World's torn apart by the inexorable forces of the cosmos!'

The senior astronaut had looked at him pityingly. 'God knows, Josh, present circumstances are enough to excuse madness in any one of us. The last few members of the human race watching their home world burn and die. Our families, our friends, everything beautiful and wonderful that our species has ever created, gone forever in an expanding ball of fire and radiation. A runaway nuclear event that we didn't foresee, couldn't control, don't understand...' he had paused to choke back the emotion engendered by his own narrative and Josh had used the moment to interrupt.

'Mad? Maybe I am mad; but at least I've found something to give purpose to my final day of life. We're the last outpost of our civilisation, here in the Martian colony, and by fate or good fortune, distant enough from the Sun to be spared for a few hours longer. And that gives me time to prepare and record everything right up to the moment ...'

'Of your own death,' finished the senior officer.

Final frame

'What's the point, man? There will be no one left to watch the thing! You'll have the dubious satisfaction of being the last human left alive, that's all, and your precious documentary will lie here until the universe itself comes to an end - and a lot of good that may do you.'

'It's a kind of immortality,' said Josh, defiantly. 'You scientists think we may be too far out to burn; that perhaps we'll just be irradiated - and that means the software may survive. Besides, it's the act that's important. Think of the orchestra playing while the Titanic sank. You could call that pointless, but those musicians will never be forgotten.'

'Until tomorrow, at around sunup,' growled Commander McCreedy. 'At which point, *everything* will be forgotten. You included.'

And with that he had bade Josh a brief farewell and had joined the rest of his crew for one last night of carousing - before, by mutual agreement, they swallowed the drugs prepared by the expedition's medic and Josh found himself alone and in sole command of the base.

He couldn't call it cowardice. By all accounts, death by radiation poisoning wasn't pleasant and without proper medical facilities, well, their suicide had pre-empted their suffering and taken them either into oblivion or some unknowable alternative. As McCreedy had observed during that last, sombre meeting, even without the radiation, there were maybe three more months before supplies ran dry, and no possibility of replenishment. A slow death from starvation; a

Five dimensional dreams

lingering one from internal bleeding and organ failure; or a chance to slip quietly into unconsciousness. No, he couldn't blame them.

He looked across to where his own allocation of the brew stood in a small flask beside the editing desk. In due course he would follow along but meanwhile there was work to do.

He checked his watch: three minutes to sunrise. He leaned forward, and read again the production notes for the final shoot.

Scene: exterior. The Martian landscape is suffused with shadows but on the far horizon a line of high, sandy cliffs is outlined with the first glimmer of light. The sun rises.

The camera was running, there was nothing more he needed to do but watch as the sun came up, blood red and huge above the escarpment and bathed the cabin in a sultry light. He waited three minutes and cut the exposure. It took him three hours to make the final edit. When he was finally satisfied with his work, he reached for the flask and removed the stopper and, as he typed the final credits, he swallowed the contents and placed the empty container carefully on the corner of his desk.

Then he leaned back in his chair and let the drug take effect. When a pleasant drowsiness had begun to fill his mind, he let his fingers find the keys for one last time and he typed: -

THE END

Divergence 2: immortal, invisible

It was after the fifth mutation that Harry fancied he saw a change in the virus's construction. Something more ordered, and, in some way he couldn't quantify, more purposeful. He mentioned it to Carstairs via video-link and received a withering response.

'We're studying a viral infection McFadian, not a bloody alien invasion.'

Then he reviewed Harry's most recent recording of capsid assembly for Covid 27, the latest coronavirus to inflict wide scale panic and misery on the world and gave his verdict in more measured tones.

'If you stare long enough at a random set of spots, your brain starts to find patterns where none exist. It's a natural tendency to seek harmony from chaos. We're all under a lot of pressure to find a vaccine for this thing and you've spent too long peering at that damn monitor. Take a couple of hours off. Go for a walk in the park. Unwind. You'll be more rational when you return, you'll see.'

Harry grunted a reply, waited for Carstairs to cut the link, and then reran the VR.

The screen showed a vague, amorphous grey cloud. From time to time, tiny blurred discs resolved from the background and quickly grew and darkened. Each was the shadow of light scattered from DNA strands of the virus and the growth reflected the formation of the protective shell of protein: the capsid. The cells he was observing were his own.

He'd been aware of the infection for several days but an innate stubbornness and a conviction that he was near to an important discovery, had kept him from following procedures and placing himself in quarantine.

Somewhere in the slurry of pixels, he felt certain, was an important truth about the evolving pathogen; and what the screen showed him was a process replicated in every part of his body.

There! That sequence had surely been more than arbitrary: a group of viruses forming and expanding in an, oh, too regular progression. He wiped a haze of sweat from his forehead with the sleeve of his lab-coat, as the picture was lost in the swirling monochrome display. And yet, even so, he felt that in that moment he suddenly understood something of the primordial drive; the restless obligation for growth and dominance; the blind and unconsidered need for control.

He stood, staggered and grasped the edge of his desk. His head spun; perspiration ran into his eyes. On the screen the dark spots had formed regimented columns, marching from left to right, and within he sensed the same army of new forms surging through his blood vessels, commanding his muscles, annexing his neural pathways.

All at once, his head cleared, the fever fell away and a new resolve took control. With carefully coordinated actions he pulled away his protective mask, stripped off his gloves and removed his coat. Beyond the confining glass-barrier the rest of the laboratory staff were going about their usual business.

Slowly and deliberately, Harry unsealed the pressurised double-doors and, as the klaxon sounded deafeningly around the facility, he stepped out and delivered his invisible cargo to their new dominion.

Double vision

Fenton pushed himself up in the bed and squinted at the clock. His eyes were gummy, blurring his vision, and it took him several attempts to bring the dial into focus.

Seven-thirty. Shit. No time to bring himself properly awake, check his phone for messages, read the news headlines – all the trivial diversions which he usually employed in order to delay the moment when he finally threw off the duvet and engaged with the mind-numbing routines of his working day.

In the bathroom, his reflected image was more than usually opaque and rubbing at the glass with his towel only resulted in further obscurity.

He peered closer; pulled down a lower eyelid to consider the revealed network of tiny blood vessels. God, he looked bad! Bloodshot didn't begin to cover it. Had he really had that much to drink last night? The memory was as indistinct as his vision – which probably meant that, yes, he'd had a skinful.

He washed perfunctorily, shaved without reference to the mirror's refracted view and quickly dressed.

As he stumbled into the kitchen the sun was rising over the distant woodland and for a moment he was blinded by the intensity of the light. He closed his eyes tight, the black arc of the after-

Five dimensional dreams

image burning in reverse across his retinas and, unsighted, crossed the room, fumbled for the cord and lowered the blind.

When he opened his eyes again, the cupboards and worksurfaces were suffused in a soft glow as the dawn light filtered through the printed fabric's weave.

Fenton hooded his eyes and waited a few moments more for his sight to fully adjust, before beginning the business of preparing breakfast.

As he reached for the cereal-packet he saw that there was still a slight fuzziness to the familiar design and he held the carton at arm's length and attempted to bring the details into proper focus. When this failed, he rubbed his eyes vigorously, wiped at the lashes with his fingers and tried again. It still didn't look quite right. Was this the booze? Or did he need bloody glasses? Christ, one night on the town couldn't age you that much, could it? He filled the bowl, replaced the box and pulled the stool up to the breakfast bar.

As he ate, he reached forward and tentatively raised the blind. The sun was already clear of the trees and it looked like it would be a nice day. He left the blind half-raised and, as he spooned cornflakes into his mouth with one hand, scrabbled around the sill with the other and located his sunglasses. That was better: with the shades on, the world looked a little less aggressive. Heck, it was bright out there, man! Even with the Ray-Bans it was hard on the old optics; and, he noticed, there was a strange effect caused no doubt by the low angle: a ghost image of a second sun,

Double vision

just below and superimposed on the first. He shrugged; like you sometimes got a second rainbow maybe – or a desert mirage. The world was full of crazy stuff.

He thumbed his phone, brought up the news pages.

Those loopy Chinese were at it again. Intent on being top nation, last week they'd launched a rocket to Mars, this week it was the test firing of their new particle accelerator. Apparently, it made the CERN version look like a Tonka Toy. Two-hundred effing miles round! Wahey! A hadron collider, that was its proper name Fenton saw, his thumb busily checking online references as he added more cornflakes to his bowl. 'Chinese to break apart the fabric of space-time' said the headline on one of the less reserved tabloids.

He left the page running and carried the empty bowl to the sink. He checked his watch; saw with consternation that he was having trouble pulling the vision from both eyes into a single coherent image. A wave of concern passed through his mind. Could alcohol damage the optic nerve? Surely not in one night? But then, perhaps it had been creeping up on him. He'd downed a few more than usual in the last couple of weeks - what with Frankie's birthday and the firm's social and last night's farewell do for Glenda.

He returned his attention to his watch. He was still experiencing double-vision but, he noted, neither over-lapping image lacked definition; what he had thought to be lack of focus was more a confusion in his mind arising from two different

Five dimensional dreams

views which couldn't be combined into one. He remembered those books of three-dimensional pictures which had been popular for a while: the one's which required you to go cross-eyed to fool the brain into merging the left and right illustrations.

He tried the method, without success, but noticed something new and strange. The two watches told slightly different times.

That couldn't be right! One eye couldn't see a different... He tried closing one eye and found he could still see two watches. This wasn't double-vision – well, not in the accepted sense. What the fuck was going on!?

He picked up his phone to repeat the observation. There was a new headline; it was almost impossible to read; he studied it carefully.

'Chinese blamed for divided realities!'

Bloody Nora! Fenton swung round urgently. 'Alexa! Read me the news.'

'Here's is the news from the BBC,' announced the speaker, obediently. *'Amidst widespread panic, Governments from around the world have blamed the Chinese research institute at Wehwing for a global phenomenon they are calling, "double vision". The recently inaugurated "Colossal Hadron Collider" in the Wehwing People's Scientific Institute of Excellence, has been held responsible for what scientists in the West are describing as a "temporal dimensional convergence event".*

'Professor Ernest Gill of the Department of Quantum Studies at Hull University explained

Double vision

that the result of this has been to superimpose two adjacent layers of reality, asynchronously. Or, put more simply, another plane of existence almost identical to our own, has been made visible to us and the match isn't perfect.

' "It's an alternative dimension which, despite its similarities, is shifted in spacetime relative to the observer," explained Professor Gill. "That means that objects which remain static in both worlds will superimpose and appear as normal, but objects which move will appear in different positions relative to each other."

'You can see a BBC graphic on our website at <u>www.bbcdoublevision/timeshift</u> which explains this more clearly.'

Fenton ran to the window, raised the blind fully and looked out onto the familiar scene. The path, the gate, the big beech tree, all looked normal. He raised his eyes up to the trees canopy. At once he could discern a lack of sharpness, a lack of distinction to the moving leaves. Beyond them the cloudless sky was a uniform blue and upon it shone two suns.

Behind him, the professor was still trying hard to explain the properties of multi-dimensional quantum physics to a bewildered and terrified population.

'You may find it easier,' he was saying, *'to compare it to a rainbow. Rainbows don't stand in one particular position. If you walk towards them, they recede and if you try circling round them, they disappear altogether. You may see a rainbow reaching the ground in a particular spot*

Five dimensional dreams

but a friend half a mile away will see the rainbow's end somewhere else altogether. That's because each rainbow is unique to the observer. Where you see it depends on where you are standing; it belongs just to you. It's a product of your own eyes.'

Fenton forced himself to turn away from the extraordinary twin suns and examine the nearby street. Things looked like they did on any normal morning. The lamppost at the corner, he was relieved to see, was sharply delineated against the morning sky; the chimneys of the adjacent houses still stood sharply angular above crisp edged roofs.

'This new, duplicate world is a little like that rainbow. Right now, we are seeing two identical worlds at the same time and a lot of what we see matches completely and looks just fine. But when you look at moving objects, say the hands of a clock, you'll find they are a second or two behind the hands of your own clock and the two positions, superimposed, will look a little blurred. Further away things will be subject to a greater shift and will be further apart in spacetime. That's why the sun in our world is higher in the sky than the sun in the newly revealed dimension.'

Across the way, old Mr Mulbury was backing his car out of his drive, just like he did every Tuesday morning. The old fool wouldn't have noticed anything was awry. Fenton doubted whether he could see clearly beyond the end of his bonnet. How he still had a driving licence at his age was a mystery. Today, his equally ancient Riley was extended by its ghostly twin, a second Mr Mulbury

Double vision

sitting crouched over the wheel, half a metre behind the first. Together they disappeared up the hill towards the traffic lights at Pound Corner. Fenton wondered, grimly, which set of lights either would observe. Indeed, it struck him that the alternative Mulbury must be living his life unaware of the new condition, otherwise he could scarcely have failed, even with his appalling eyesight, to have seen his doppelganger seated just along his bonnet.

He wondered too, whether the second Mr M might stop at a red light in his own dimension, while Fenton's neighbour, approaching an earlier green, would clear the crossing and thus separate himself from his dimensional twin. In that way, he mused, the pair might move further apart throughout the day and only resume their closer liaison when one climbed back into bed with the other; following an identical series of movements but never quite in tandem.

So, what were the ramifications of the Chinese' interference with the proper laws of nature? Could life continue as before or would one dimension become hopelessly entangled with the other, making co-existence impossibly confusing?

Fenton, his brain in a whirl, turned from the window, almost struck his head on the open cupboard door, reached out to shut it, knowing he had already done so, and found his hand moving through empty space.

Already his two worlds were moving further apart. Those last moments spent in introspection, had been enough to cause divergence. A metre

Five dimensional dreams

away, another, uncomprehending Fenton, living his life minutes later, had moved to the breakfast bar and was reaching for his sunglasses.

As Fenton watched, the other occupant of the kitchen started at some sound and looked across to the stairs, where a third figure descended, blinking, into the sunlight.

The new arrival ignored them both. Eyes screwed shut against the glare, he fumbled past his astonished twin and lowered the blind.

Despite these actions, the view of the morning sky, Fenton saw, was still quite clear and from it shone three suns.

From above, he heard the distinct sound of a tap being turned on in the bathroom.

Who's counting?

'A countdown to death,' I said, securing the airlock and decoupling my helmet seal, 'that's what it amounts to – from the moment they're born. Dammit! It must affect every action they take for the rest of their lives.'

'Not necessarily,' Harry replied, stowing his suit and crossing to the synth. 'They probably don't give it a thought until the last couple of years. Like us, I imagine they just get on with it. My father made it to a hundred-and four and he was studying Spanish when he died! At that age you can't be sure each day isn't your last, but that didn't stop him.'

'That's just my point,' I said, stashing my own gear and joining him at the counter, *'you can't be sure*. Maybe you'll die tomorrow and maybe you won't. Even at a hundred-and-four you might have another year or two in you, so why not enjoy yourself while you can? Average life expectancy on Earth is still around ninety-six so your dad got an eight-year bonus! That's long enough to learn Chinese if the fancy takes you.'

He grinned, collected his meal from the dispenser and took a seat at the cabin's central diner.

'So, it's just a matter of planning,' he suggested.

We'd been on Fubar Major for two weeks, Old Temporal, and talks with the Farn were proceeding sluggishly. We'd established contact with the ruling elite, developed a language-trove from which the IT guys upstairs had constructed

Five dimensional dreams

workable translation software and were attempting to kick-start discussions on possible trade and cultural exchange.

I had shuttled down to install the necessary communications software and had, in the process, become a bystander to a moment in history, the Farn being the first sentient race which a century of interstellar travel had unearthed.

'They start the powwow proper tomorrow,' I volunteered, 'if that's what you mean. Apparently, the Farn are annoyingly unresponsive to setting targets but I understand that the first thing on the agenda is to establish a proper name for the place; find out how the locals want their planet to be referred to from here-on-in.'

'Before they find out what we *have* been calling it,' said Harry, taking a seat opposite and forking a generous helping of proweave into his mouth.

I chuckled and sliced into my own steak. The current designation on the charts made use of a term devised when my father had been a boy: an acronym for, "Fucked Up Beyond All Recognition" and placed there by the first team to properly plot the world's position and status, an earlier error in mapping having recorded it as, "a cometary object". By the time anyone in authority found out, the name was on a hundred data bases.

The Farn was what the natives called themselves and it seemed likely that Farn's World, or something similar, would be the new moniker when talks resumed.

'That thing about knowing when you'll die,' I said, returning to our previous conversation, 'you think

Who's counting

it just means that you make your plans accordingly, allow for the time you have left? That it gives you the opportunity to tie things up properly, is that it?'

The ship's xenoanthropologist pushed his plate aside and took a long pull of what the synth liked to term "beer". 'Look,' he said, looking serious for once, 'according to the guys on the First Contact mission, every Farn knows the precise day on which they will die. Evolution has given them an exact life-term, after which, their bodies cease to function. It's the same amount of time for each and every one of them. The organ that passes for a heart in each Farn is programmed to beat for a precise number of times and that's it, caput! And, it seems, from the moment they're capable of conscious thought, they're given that information: "Hey fella! This is when you're gonna die!"

'It would have to be something genetic,' he continued, 'a chance mutation that just happened to be useful. Maybe there was pressure for space or food and smaller numbers were advantageous to survival; not an individual benefit, but something that would help everyone. It couldn't be passed on by natural selection; you can't breed when you're dead!'

'The point is they've turned dying into a lifestyle!' I said. 'I understand there's a day - when they're still wet behind the ears - when they have a special ceremony, with singing and fireworks and get presented with a tag to wear round their neck that has the date of their death etched into it! Don't tell me that doesn't have an effect on their mental wellbeing.'

'It's what seems to be going on but the details are sketchy,' Harry protested. 'Something may have been lost in translation.'

'OK, so maybe there are no fireworks,' I spread my hands in a "so what" gesture, 'but that sell-by date must be a big thing – not just something they worry about in their final few weeks.'

'Alright,' he conceded, 'but if it's always been that way, society will have adjusted to it. It may be that they just take it as read and get on with their lives.'

Harry climbed to his feet and took both our plates and rammed them into the recycler; later they would be part of our evening meal.

'Personally,' I said, after a moment, 'I've always imagined that I'll live forever, and I'll go on imagining that until I die. Wanting to keep living is what makes us human; we fight till the last breath in our bodies,' I looked up and caught his eye, 'and meanwhile,' I said, 'we learn Spanish.'

Like I said, I was just a programmer and only an onlooker to the main event but I recalled Harry's words a few days later when the Farn's senior negotiator died between sessions.

In any normal scenario it would have been an occasion for shock and commiserations but, the delegation from Earth was forced to reminded itself, according to Harry, the event had been foreseen a lifetime before.

In which case, why hadn't the Farn warned us of his impending death? Why hadn't he stood aside and let them appoint another, younger representative, in his place. Why, if he knew he was unable to complete the round of talks, had he come forward at all?

'I'm wondering,' said Harry, who had taken to using me as a sounding board for his musings, 'whether it's some sort of believe fulfilment. You know, like the Vikings dying in battle: maybe it's important for the Farn to die in harness. Show no fear, that sort of thing.'

'Or you were right before and they just don't think it's important enough to disturb their daily routine,' I suggested. 'An interesting proposition if you're flying a plane or conducting brain surgery.'

Although, I thought, those weren't problems they'd been faced with yet; the Farn had only the simplest of lifestyles and a frustrating disinterest in engaging in discussion concerning the future relationship of our two species, even though it was they who were most likely to benefit from the exchange.

As the ship's single xenoanthropologist, Harry was in the firing line. What exactly was it he had missed, the senior members of our delegation wanted to know? If these annoying aliens were aware of their impending demise, why had they foisted their most geriatric member onto our discussions?

The question wasn't entirely reasonable of course; xenoanthropology was in its infancy, the Farn being the first subjects available for study. Assessing the mores and motives of an entire race of extra-terrestrials was a daunting enough task given years of investigation; uncovering their

Five dimensional dreams

secrets in a matter of days was nigh impossible. So, perhaps the delegation was as surprised as I was when Harry came up with the answer.

'It's those damned tags they wear round their necks,' he explained to me later, after he had presented his latest research to the senior delegates. 'I was looking at the recordings of the first session - when the Farn leader introduced himself - and I remembered something that came up in our conversation.'

'*Our* conversation?'

'Yes, when you described the ceremony in which the tags are awarded, and I said, maybe something got lost in translation.'

'Oh, that. And did it?'

'Yes, I blew up a still and took a look at the Farn's particular tag and that's when I realised my mistake.'

'Which was?' I asked.

'Well, the tag didn't carry a date and time. 'it didn't show the day or the hour the Farn delegate died.'

'Ha! So, you got it wrong! What *was* on the tag then - a reminder of his mother's birthday?'

Harry laughed dutifully. 'No, and that's where the confusion came in. The literal translation is, "predictive death tag" and given the Farn's unique lifecycle, I jumped to the conclusion that it showed the date of their death; but the term turns out to be a mite misleading. In this case it only said that the days of his life were circumscribed! And I believe that every tag carries the same information. It seems that the Farn simply wear it as a symbol of

Who's counting

their mortality. They don't know *when* they'll die any more than you and I.'

'But surely,' I insisted, 'all they need to do is add their known lifespan to their date of birth and...?' I hesitated, because Harry was shaking his head.

'What season is it on Fubar?' he asked, in what seemed like a clumsy attempt to change the subject.

'Er, I dunno, I haven't given it much thought. What the hell has that got to do...ah, you mean...'

'No axial tilt!' nodded Harry, waiting for me to get two and two to add up to four. I still couldn't see the connection and gave him a puzzled look.

'No tilt, no seasons. No seasons, no repetitive weather events to mark the cycle of the year. No obvious way to divide the passage of time.'

'There's still day and night,' I observed.

'But nothing to distinguish each from the ones that went before. The point is the Farn don't experience time like we do. It doesn't occur to them to mark anniversaries. Events occur and are remembered but not in any regular pattern. There's no concept of, "the same time next year." There's no concept of "year" in anything but a purely astronomical sense. The Farn have never developed a calendar. Things happened in the past and new things will happen in the future, but they don't link them mentally, the way you and I do.'

'As with birthdays,' I said, finally getting a handle on the conversation.

'Exactly! They don't have them, and they wouldn't understand what you meant if you asked them how old they are.'

Five dimensional dreams

'Right, so although every Farn lives for a quite precise period of time, none of 'em knows when the end will come.'

'No, and that way, you might expect, they avoid that terrible anxiety and lack of purpose we spoke about. You might wonder if Farn society subconsciously suppresses an awareness of passing time in order to protect its citizens from just such pressures.'

'And so, the senior delegate's death...?'

'Was totally unexpected, which sets up a whole new array of considerations.'

'It does?'

'If you consider that there is no lingering old age on Fubar. You don't sit around watching daytime holocasts in your dotage. As far as we can see, the Farns' lifespan ends abruptly, while they are still, to all other intents, hale and hearty. Imagine waiting for that to catch up with you.'

'Especially,' I said, 'if you don't know how old you are. Every moment could be your last. But come on, they must have at least a ballpark figure regarding their age. They must be aware of which generation they represent; they must see their near contemporaries reaching the ends of *their* lives; and then they must know that their own death can't be too far off. You'd think that would be an incentive to achieve as much as possible in the time remaining and yet, ambition seems to be an unknown concept on Fubar. Do you reckon you might have lost something – in translation?'

Harry had the good grace to look suitably abashed.

Who's counting

'You've seen the Farn,' he countered. 'Rigid chitinous exoskeletons; heads like rusty iron castings with ball-bearing eyes. Age isn't something you can easily determine. And they don't have strong familial ties. Farn society is made up of disparate groups of individuals who have similar interests. The young move between collectives until their career path is decided by committee. By the time they are fully mature it's quite probable that they have no inkling of which stage in their lifecycle they've reached.'

'In which case, having a precisely finite lifespan isn't significant,' I concluded. 'Is it?'

Harry fixed me with the sort of look my old Lifesciences tutor used to employ when he thought my attention had been wandering.

'There are no elderly Farn,' he said, patiently. 'That pre-determined cut-off point arrives when the individual is at the height of their mental and physical powers. And although they don't know when it will occur, they know for certain that it will. How then can they make any plans for the future? How can they retain desire and intent?'

I didn't hazard a reply. I just adopted a neutral expression and waited for him to supply the answer.

'Like the Farn,' he said, after a long pause, 'you and I don't know when we will die. But unlike them, we do expect some prior warning - a slow deterioration in our health, a diagnosed condition, advancing old age. Yes, a few of us drop dead unexpectedly, but that's the significant word, "unexpectedly". For the Farn it's *always* expected.

Five dimensional dreams

The ironic thing is that in a race which has a fully determinable moment of death, no one has the information to make the calculation! And so, they wake up every day unaware of whether they will see tomorrow.'

'Which is surely why there's been no equivalent of the Industrial Revolution on Fubar,' I said, 'no Age of Enlightenment. How can you engage in R&D when you have no interest in the outcome? Unless perhaps, you are working for the benefit of others.'

Harry smiled, grimly. 'Progress is seldom driven by altruism. To a large extent, our own civilisation grew on personal ambition, self-interest and greed. Sometimes it was a simple desire for knowledge but generally, that knowledge was used by others to attain fame and fortune. The Farn's lack of purpose has at least spared them that.'

So, is there any point in continuing the talks?' I asked. 'Can the Farn find any value in them.'

'I'm told we might be able to re-engineer their genome and make their lifespan less predictable. But I doubt that they'd be willing to exchange one uncertainty for another. Where's the gain?'

'Or,' I suggested after a long moment's consideration, 'we could just get them to register their births and exchange that neck-tag for a proper digital count-down, although I don't imagine they'd see that as an improvement either.'

'Almost certainly,' said Harry, 'the Farn would see their situation as superior to yours and mine; and who's to say they'd be wrong. There's no competition between them, no conflict. None of that insatiable drive for dominance which has been so destructive for the human race.'

'It's taken us to the stars,' I said.

'So it has.'

Harry stood quietly for a moment, gazing out through the viewport onto the Farn's untroubled home world. 'I'll tell you one thing,' he said at last, without turning his head, 'they may not be passionate or aspirational but they're one thing we will never be.'

'And what's that?' I asked.

He turned and smiled ruefully.

'Content,' he said. 'Content.'

Five dimensional dreams

Skin deep

'You want to *adopt* a *HUMAN?* By Wastorm's toadmember! Are you mad!?'

'Well, maybe not adopt, that's probably the wrong term, but *mentor* then – yes, mentor; that's a better way to put it.'

'It doesn't matter which way you put it: *you can't do it!* I'm not having one of those things setting up home in my clam case!'

'Oh, Flem! Fensle said that would be the way you'd react and I told her you were more progressive than she realised.'

'Ha! Fensle. I might have guessed she was behind this ridiculous scheme – and I *am* progressive - when it concerns something sensible, that will bring benefits to the community.'

'Well, there you are then. Bringing a human into the collective will have all sorts of rewards...'

'Such as?'

'Broadening our understanding of...things. Getting a new perspective on...um...'

'Ha! You see! You're already struggling to justify this idiotic plan. And besides, what makes you think a human would *want* to merge with The Reef Spontaneity anyway? From what I've heard, these *homo sapiens* are pretty independent; keep

Five dimensional dreams

themselves to themselves. Haven't noticed too many of them turning up at the weekly meld, that's for sure!'

'Flem! That's just silly! They're hardly likely to swim over one evening and join you and your cronies for a moult. For a start, they're much too polite to arrive without an invitation and anyway – well, I don't think they do moult, do they?'

'Shouldn't think so; underneath all that protective clothing they're a revolting mass of soft blubber – and before you ask, I absorbed a co-mingle on the subject, the swell before yesterday. Opened my eyes to what humans are all about, I can tell you.'

'Ah! Out it comes at last! The *real* reason you don't like my suggestion: narrow-minded, species prejudice. Fensle was right. "A mass of soft blubber" indeed! Except for the lack of an exoskeleton, humans are just like you and me.'

'You *are* joking? Have you seen one without its environment suit? All those orifices! And that stuff they call "hair", for Vimprox sake! What's that all about, eh?'

'Oh, that's only an evolutionary detail. Their ancestors left the sea eons ago; they're bound to *look* different. That doesn't mean they *think* differently.'

'Well, I wouldn't trust them. Shifty eyes I say. It's those peculiar skin flaps – lids I believe they call them. Give me a decent eyestalk any day. You can tell what a fella's thinking with a proper ommatophore.'

'Damscertle! You're hopeless! As if the shape of

Skin deep

your eye matters in the greater scheme of things. I've no doubt they feel all the same emotions as us Ventrons: happiness; sadness; love...'

'Hate. Yeah, well I wouldn't let my spawn marry one, that's for sure – and talking about spawn, what *is* Fensle up to these days – when she isn't plotting the take-over of my household by aliens, that is.'

'Oh, she's been spending some time over in the shallows with her friends.'

'The shallows? You mean where the humans have their habitation pods? Sounds risky. Watch out they don't net her and use her for a laboratory specimen.'

'Ha - ha. They're not primitives, Flem. In fact, they've asked her to help with some of their research. It'll all count towards her finals next year. She's getting on really well with one of their marine biologists; he says she's a natural.'

'I'll bet he does! Seriously Marli, we know very little about these creatures and their motivations. This biologist guy is bound to have an agenda; I don't imagine he's got the hots for our girl, do you! I mean, given that he's soft and pink and a couple of daisoes long and she's hard-shelled and green and at least a torg from tail to...'

'Flem! Stop it! What do you know about your daughter's feelings? When have you ever shown an interest in her friends? Who're you to judge – anyone? What do you know about love!'

'...Love? *Love?* **LOVE!!?** Trenkle's jebbit! This is what this '*adoption*' fiasco is all about! You're trying to give Professor Blob up there, a free pass

55

Five dimensional dreams

into my daughter's private recess!'

'That's absurd! It's purely an academic friendship. And if he *does* join us here, I'll make up a separate fissure for his personal use. Of course, he'll need to bring his own oxygen...'

'Heavy breather, is he? No, no, OK, alright, I'm sorry, but look, Marli, you've got to give me this; I know better than you what a young man's after when he's lonely and a long way from home - and believe me, it isn't sea shells.'

'Flem, I really think it's a union of minds, you know. Can't you look beyond his physical appearance and see what Fensle sees?'

'No. You and Fensle are both blinkered when it comes to our extra-terrestrial friends. I'm the only one seeing the wider picture. If you want my opinion these humans are overrated, over-eager and over here and the sooner they get back to their own arm of the galaxy, the better.'

'They're just sentient beings, like the rest of us, Flem.'

'Well, they're not like me, and I want to see Fensle back here before third tide; am I making myself clear?'

'As a conch. But you'll have to get her yourself. Last time we spoke, she was planning to spend the next drift in the humans' observation tank; to be near Harry.'

'HARRY? Who the...oh...damn she was!

'He seems very sweet natured.'

'And just how would you know that? ...you don't mean that you've **met** him?'

'Well, you know, just to say "Hi!".

Skin deep

' "Just to say...!" Am I the *only* crustacean trying to maintain standards around here?'

'Flem – that's unfair. Some of your best friends are gastropods, What about Bryni?'

'Bryni? Yeah, well, he's...OK. Yeah, he's a pal; a regular guy.'

'Exactly. Look, Fensle's happy and isn't that what matters? Let her make her own life, wherever she chooses.'

'Yeah, maybe. Do you suppose she'll go back with them, Marl? Earth, I think they call their place. Do you think we'll ever see our girl again?'

'Why don't you swim over to the shallows and ask her, Flem?

'Yeah, I could, I suppose; swim over. Hey...Marl?'
Yes, Flem.'

'Do you think you could rustle-up a moules marinier maybe. You know, just in case I invite anyone back for supper. I mean, you never know. Maybe he's a regular guy.'

'Yes, Flem, maybe he is.

Five dimensional dreams

Time passing

'There – is – no - paradox!'

Professor Mitchell Humble threw his arms out to left and right, the fingers of each hand spread, assertively.

'But Mitchell, what about the old, "shoot your grandfather" argument. That must still hold good, surely?'

On the other side of the fire, his friend grimaced theatrically and sank back into his armchair. 'I don't think you've understood a word I've said, have you?' he volunteered, reaching for the drink resting on a side-table.

'Well,' replied the other, 'I wouldn't go that far. I followed you up to the "temporal interphase cross-dimensional" - thingy. After that? No, didn't have the faintest idea what you were on about.'

Mitchell grinned. 'Nothing new there then. What did you get for physics 'O' Level? Ungraded?'

'Almost certainly would have done if I old Gormenghast hadn't sensibly transferred me to the biology lab. *"Cut up a few frogs, Carter, I think it's an activity more suited to your temperament".*'

'And did you become a famous anatomist...?'

'No, I joined the bank and made myself filthy rich. Never saw the appeal of the sciences; labouring for the furtherance of knowledge. Mugs' game – present company excepted.'

Mitchell bowed his head in acceptance of the grudging exclusion. 'A BSc is certainly no

Five dimensional dreams

guarantee of a healthy bank balance – unless you make a major breakthrough in your field of study.'

'And you reckon you have? Made a breakthrough? In, er, temporary cross-dressing?' It was Pat's turn to grin. 'You see, I *was* listening.'

Mitchell laughed, took a swig of his whisky and placed the glass carefully back onto the table.

'Cross-dimensional temporal interphase,' he said, enunciating each word carefully for his companion's full edification. 'Time travel, to the uneducated masses – present company excluded.'

'Yes, I did get the general implication. And I repeat, what about the paradoxes implicit in the activity. What *does* happen if you travel back and shoot your grandpa before he meets your gran? So that your parents are never born and –'

Mitchell raised his hands again, this time palms out, to halt the enquiry. 'Yes, OK, I've heard the argument before. Most recently from you; and I repeat, there is no paradox; no two irreconcilable states of being. A moment in time is always just that. A single point in the temporal mix; inextricably linked to events around it.'

'But that's just the point – sorry, no pun intended – what happens anywhere in your time stream affects what happens later, er, further *down*stream. Doesn't it?'

'Most certainly. But you've got to forget this "flowing river of time" idea. If you are going to accept the concept of travelling *through* time, you've got to accept too that there *is* no past, no future; just events.'

'But there's still cause and effect?'

Time passing

'Oh yes. The narrative still has a logical sequence. Like a book which you read from left to right, even though the entire content exists all of the time. Chapter one is still there when you reach the last page, but the beginning and end of the story are the sum of all the events in between. Still with me?'

Pat nodded, uncertainly. 'And, if you went back and rewrote chapter two, the end would still be the same?'

'Now you're thinking like a scientist! Yes, that's where the book analogy breaks down. It's like comparing mixing paint colours with the light spectrum. They're chalk and cheese - sorry, too many comparisons! But time isn't like the printed page. If you shoot your forebear then you *will* prevent your own birth.'

'Ha! Paradox alert! Wasn't that shot aimed at your own foot Mitchell? If you prevent familial rogering at the prescribed moment in your history, then you won't be around to go back and murder Grandad Humble. Quod et demonstrandum and all that!'

'Erat, Pat. It's erat. And you're wrong. The thing is you *do* exist and shooting all your ancestors back to 1066 won't alter that fact. But,' Mitchell continued, hurriedly, as he saw Pat open his mouth to object, 'wiping out your family *will* prevent your birth somewhere in the continuum. Shooting your forebear has a relationship to what brought the act about and to his absence from the narrative. But although cause and effect are immutable, they are not consecutive. Granddad

Five dimensional dreams

lies dead on the living room carpet and so, he must get shot, somewhere on that particular temporal pathway.'

Pat looked up, opened his mouth to speak, shut it again and studied the carpet for several minutes. Mitchell sat back, sipped at his whisky and waited patiently while his friend grappled with the concept.

'You're saying,' said Pat, at last, 'that there is really no before and after, and that everything exists, *simultaneously*?'

Mitchell laughed, 'Yes, and that applies to all alternative scenarios too. 'The *Infiniverse* I like to call it. Time isn't a river at all; it's a multidimensional ocean in which everything that can happen, *is* happening – synchronously!'

'But, that's crazy! There must be zillions of alternative possibilities every second!'

'Oh, more than zillions. We're talking *infinite* here, Pat. This is monkeys-typing-Shakespeare country - and while they're at it, randomly creating every other work of literature and the Yellow Pages too! So, while we are arguing the toss here in your ostentatious abode, my grandfather already lies dead on the kitchen floor and I am both setting out to do the deed and returning with the smoking revolver. Unless...'

'Unless what?'

'Unless my time machine doesn't work. I mean, I personally have no murderous intent towards my predecessors but once the device exists then the infinite outcomes rule dictates that I will, in one dimension or the other, do the deed.'

Time passing

'If everything is possible, isn't time travel inevitable anyway?'

'Ha! No, the infiniverse doesn't permit magic! Extraordinary as it may be, it still operates within the usual laws of physics. If travel between temporal pathways proves to be impossible, then impossible it is.'

'If it *is* possible – and I have every faith in your scientific skills – wouldn't we know? Wouldn't your "infinite outcomes rule" mean that someone utilising the device would have visited us already?'

'You're having trouble with that word "infinite" again. There will be dimensions where that has happened and others where they won't have turned up – and this may be - clearly is - one of them.'

'Alright, enough of the "Idiots' guide to temporal physics", let's get down to practicalities. When do you set off?'

Mitchell stood, flexed his shoulders to restore circulation to cramped muscles and carried his empty glass to the window. Outside, the Sussex countryside rolled away from the house in an extravagance of green.

'You make it sound like an expedition to the Amazon!' he said, in an attempt to lighten his own growing concerns. 'I don't see it as "setting off" so much as "blending into" a different plane of existence. There won't be any travelling involved – not geographically anyway.'

'The important thing with any journey,' remarked Pat, ignoring the physical nature of the enterprise,

Five dimensional dreams

'is to have mapped out the return leg. If you need to, can you get back, in a hurry?'

'The pulse generator should hold the wave in stasis for three minutes,' said Mitchell, as much to assure himself as to answer his friend's question. 'When it breaks down, I'll return to my starting point; or, in a very real sense, my starting point will return to me. I only intend to "step sideways" on this initial venture – a short way into the future, if you insist on thinking of it that way. I could give you the formulae if you'd be interested.'

'Ha ha. Very droll. Look, I'm not so keen on that "should hold". Is there an element of doubt?'

'In every task that must be done, Pat. I've checked my calculations a hundred times; I'm as certain as possible that it will work. I've asked you along to witness a moment in history, not to man the lifeboats.'

'These are waters in which I cannot row, Mitchell. And, that's why I brought along a bottle of best malt. You said when you called that your demonstration would be a Nobel Prize moment and I can finance a celebratory bottle of Rare Cask, if I'm good for nothing else.'

Mitchell moved from the window and replaced his glass on the table. 'And I'm grateful, Pat. You've already bolstered my resolve. Come on, let's get the show on the road,' and so saying, he walked over to a doughnut-shaped device set up in the centre of the room.

It most resembled a large electrical coil with cylindrical attachments and a small control panel

Time passing

linked to the body of the equipment by a thin cable.

'Anything I can do?' asked Pat, without expectation of a positive response. He was not disappointed.

'Keep well clear,' replied his friend, stepping into the centre of the circle and stooping to retrieve the controls. 'I don't think the field extends much beyond the framework but I don't want any unintended passengers. Well, here goes; wish me luck,' and he thumbed an in-set button causing a suitably dramatic red glow to rise from the surrounding equipment and enfold his body in a pulsing aura of light.

After a moment, in which his eyes adjusted to the odd illumination, Pat could see that Mitchell no longer stood within the pulsating column. He checked his watch; three minutes Mitchell had said, before the projection subsided and the scientist returned to the study. Or, if he took Mitchell's observations as literal, the study returned to him.

It crossed his mind at once, that if this exchange of locations was indeed organised in that manner, then it was he, and the study and his entire dimension which were shifting position and leaving Mitchell behind to await the instantaneous arrival of whichever plan of existence he had chosen to visit. The thought was disturbing. Suddenly, he *was* a part of the experiment, whatever Mitchell had said regarding the machine's field of influence.

Five dimensional dreams

He looked towards the windows again and let his eye follow the patchwork of fields south, to where a faded blue ridge marked the position of the distant Downs. It all looked comfortingly familiar – and why wouldn't it? If the states of existence were infinite, then there must be any number which were indistinguishable from this one. He trawled deep into his memory for an appropriate fact. Infinity, he felt sure he had learned, long ago, was indivisible and so, didn't that mean that any part of infinity was infinite too? Could you even have a half share of infinity? He experienced a moment of intellectual vertigo. It was like trying to get your head around that old conundrum about the endless universe and what contained it. Most people could spot the oxymoron but they still sought to form a picture in their head which would be illogically satisfying. Some said it proved the existence of God; others that it simply proved the lack of processing power in the human brain. In his case, he bowed to the latter opinion but acknowledged that some, like Mitchell, were equipped to wrestle with the concept and see at least the shadow of an answer.

His watch showed that two minutes had passed. He studied the second hand as it crawled, remorselessly around the dial. He was aware, in his peripheral vision, that he had moved nearer to the wave generator and, as the watch counted down the last few moments, his arm brushed the rose-red light, the pulsing movement stopped dead, and something like the tingle of a mild electric shock crawled over his body as whatever

Time passing

process the coil had powered was arrested by his interference.

And in that instant, he finally understood infinity; saw with a fearsome clarity the awful nature of its being; felt it engulf his soul and, in doing so, deny his lack of intellect and reveal the truth of creation.

Half a metre and a galaxy away, Mitchell waited for the wave to die and return him to his own point in time and space. He knew of infinity but was not granted an insight into its shape and purpose; and so, he waited; and waited; and waited...

Divergence 3: pork scratchings

Them wild boar had been scratching and raking at the door of the barn for nearly a week afore granddad took up his shotgun and fired clean through the timbers and blinded the big male and killed one of the youngsters outright. The rest ran off a bit and eyed us careful like, when we opened up and dragged in the carcass, and the big old brute he just stood there with his flanks heavin' and blood pouring down his snout and gatherin' round his great, curved tusks and Daddy swung the rusty mattock that had hung from the barn wall fer as long as I could remember and split his skull wide open.

That would have bin about the third year of the war and so mebbe the fifth year since the plague started up and so, therefore, near to the year 2075 in the old reckonin'.

Them pigs fed us fer a fair few months and that was about the best eatin' I kin remember up till I was a man.

Most of the time we went hungry. Course, we'd set traps up all through the wood but the defoliants had done fer most of the trees and the deer was cleaned out right at the start, when the virus drove everyone out of the towns and inta the countryside. Things were pretty desperate even afore the fightin' begun and afterwards, well there weren't so many of us left to make a livin' off the land, which was just as well I suppose.

Pork scratchings

We picked up enough to scrape along back then: squirrel made a decent enough casserole, and a badger was a poor but palatable substitute fer the wild boar. Fox could be eaten, but it was tough and sinewy and stunk real bad during cookin'. Other than that, there were plenty of leaves and roots, if you knew what you were about; and berries and nuts where the bushes had survived. Further out you could still find a farm field that had been left to run wild and once or twice Ma managed to grind up a flour and bake what she told us was called bread.

What you gotta realise is that we boys didn't know no better and so we didn't feel deprived – nor the girls neither I guess. That was how life had always bin and we got on and enjoyed it when we could and hunkered down and made do when we couldn't.

Fer our parents and fer granddad specially, it musta bin different, cos they could remember the old times when they all lived in the big city and there was some kind of magic in the air, or so they said. They told tales on long winter nights but in truth, we didn't pay too much heed; it all sounded far-fetched and at any rate, a long way beyond recoverin'.

They didn't know why there was a war but thought mebbe we was just caught up in the crossfire. Anyways, by that time the virus was out and folks were dyin' in their thousands and there was no news coming through.

One thing I do remember was one night when the barn was all in shadows and the fire had been lit in

Five dimensional dreams

the middle of the floor and the blue wood-smoke was windin' its way up to th' gap in the tiles high above our heads, and Granddad started to talk about the old times and he said, it was the way mankind was and we had no one to blame but ourselves. He said that the world was going to pot long afore the war or even the plague and that thinnin' out the population was about the best thing that could have happened; and I looked across to Ma to see if she agreed and I saw the light from the fire reflected in a tear, just afore she wiped it away and smiled across to where I was sittin'.

Pork scratchings

Amateur dramatics

'Houston, we have a problem.'

Alex Burnside's lip curled in derision. Space tourists! If he'd realised how many times he'd be subjected to that spurious quotation, he'd have fought harder against the commercialisation of NASA's space programme. Riled, he thumbed aggressively at the response button.

'ISS, this is Houston. Tell us your problem.'

He reached for a pen, scribbled, "*Little green men"* on a Post-it and, leaning across fixed it to the monitor screen of the Assistant Flight Commander, Jeff Cornski.

Cornski grinned and copying his action wrote, "*WCS*" on his own note pad, thrust his hand into his pants' pocket, withdrew a dollar and placed the coin and the note on the corner of Burnside's desk.

Burnside gestured his agreement. The station's Waste Collection System was certainly the piece of equipment which gave rise to more alarm and uncertainty than any other, during what they termed contemptuously, "holiday bookings".

He was about to acknowledge the fact and return the bet to his colleague's desk when the answer to his request came through on the control-room speakers.

'Houston, we have a visitor.'

He looked across at Cornski. Cornski shook his head, despairingly.

'ISS, please repeat.'

Amateur dramatics

'Houston, we have a visitor.'

Burnside pulled out his wallet, withdrew a twenty-dollar bill and placed it on the note.

Cornski smiled and switched on his own microphone. 'Roger that ISS. Is he small and green?'

Burnside stifled a snigger, set Cornski chuckling and a moment later they both dissolved into silent laughter.

'He's pretty small but more off-white than green. I guess you'd say, sallow. Look Houston, I'm not sure you understand the gravity of the situation. We have a problem up here. Please advise. The Commander and other personnel are in lockdown in the storage facility. There's just Betty and me – I'm Gregory Hayward the owner of TransOcean Airways by the way, and there's just us and...the visitor.'

Burnside wiped a handkerchief across his eyes and sat up straight.

'Roger that Mr Hayward. Can you describe your visitor?'

'Yes Houston, like I told you, he's short, pale-skinned, dark haired.'

'And are there any other distinguishing features?'

Burnside frowned and waved Cornski away, as the AFC dangled the Twenty-dollar note mockingly in his line of sight.

'There's a flag on the shoulder of his spacesuit. I don't recognise the design. Maybe it's North Korea.'

Burnside was on his feet in an instant. Cornski dropped the bank note and grabbed a phone.

Five dimensional dreams

'Roger that Mr Hayward. Has he made any demands?

'He wants to know if we have any tea.'

'Mr Hayward, did you say "tea"?

'That's right...and a digestive biscuit.'

'Does he have *a weapon* Mr Hayward. How did he overpower the crew?'

A digestive biscuit? Who the hell...? To his right, Cornski was shouting urgently into the phone.

'Hello Houston. He didn't overpower anyone. The crew were all in storage facility 3 dealing with a technical malfunction and the door was sealed automatically when our visitor opened the central airlock. Betty and I are in Module Six and we're conversing with him via the internal comms system.'

'Conversing? Does he speak English?'

'After a fashion, yes.'

'If he's in touch via the comms system we should be able to patch him through,' said Cornski, switching extensions and shouting instructions into the mouthpiece. A moment later a new voice issued from the speakers.

'A'right Wack, 'ow're yez doin', son?'

Burnside sat down again, heavily. Was that North Korean? He didn't think so. It sounded vaguely familiar. 'Who am I speaking to?' he asked.

'Yozzer Hughes, me old mucker.'

Perhaps it *was* Korean. He found himself stuttering. 'H...H...How the hell did you get onboard?'

'Frun dure. Dead simple. Yez wanna watch that.

74

Amateur dramatics

Anybody c'd turn op on yez step.'

'But... how? I mean, what...that is who took you up?'

'Oor Jason's rocket, man. Worked a treat.'

'Who by all that's holy are "Ewer-Jason"?' Burnside looked across at Cornski who shrugged his shoulders and began tapping at his keyboard. There were independent conglomerates all over the damn globe who were trying to get in on commercial spaceflight, and several had working rocket systems under trial; but he knew most of them by name and the idea that some anonymous organisation might have developed anything sophisticated enough to rendezvous with the ISS *and* gain entry without all the necessary protocols, was the stuff of dreams.

'Not "who *are*" son, "who *is*".' The voice sounded slightly indignant, and re-emphasised its original response. 'Oo-er Jas-on. He built his rocket in me gran's backyar' – mind yez, she runs an engineerin' company see.

'But...' Burnside was momentarily lost for words. 'The fuel, the pressure suits the...the...,' heck, you couldn't just build a functioning spacecraft in your yard! This had to be a scam.

'There's bags o' stuff knocking aroun' online if ye nah wuz ter look, like. Oor kid's sound as a pound whun it comes ter engineerin'.'

Cornski, who had been busy communicating the incident upline, signed for his colleague's attention and spoke in a stage whisper. 'The Deputy Administrator has spoken to the White House. They say, "there's no evidence of the North Koreans developing space-capable flight systems at

Five dimensional dreams

this time," unquote. Meanwhile, they are mobilising all necessary agencies and advise we keep talking until the Chief Administrator arrives.'

Burnside pulled a face and turned back to the console.

'How did you get onboard?' he asked, in an attempt to gain control of the conversation. 'The entry lock requires very specific docking procedures with complex algorithms to ensure the integrity of the pressure seals.'

'Oh yeah, me gran was workin' on that fer days. Got the plans frum "Engineerin' Weekly" and oor kid hacked in ter yez files fer the over-rides. Dead simple, like. Yous wanna tighten up yer security me owd wack.'

'You over-rode the...!' Burnside reached for the plastic cup on his desk and took a long swallow of water. 'Just where are you from?'

'Norris Green.'

'Say again.' It didn't sound like "North Korea" but with the strange accent it was difficult to be entirely sure.

'Norris Green, Liverpool, England. Look, wack, it's been nice chattin' but I've gorra get back. Places ter go, people ter see, you know how it is, son.'

'Go? Go where? You've only just arrived! Isn't that the point of your mission?'

'Gerraway! We juss stopped off ter be polite and gerra cup o' char, like. We're on us way ter Lunar Base.'

Burnside widened his eyes and ran a hand through what remained of his hair. 'Lunar Base?

Amateur dramatics

We haven't got a Lunar Base,' he said, the suddenly predictable response half formed in his mind before the actual one issued from the speakers.

'*Yous* haven't gorra Lunar Base, sunshine; but me owd Gran, now that's a different matter.'

Divergence 4: seascape

Fedra adjusted the UV shutters and tilted the sun bed so that her head and shoulders were in the shade cast by the solar roof panel. Temperatures were predicted to reach 45°c by noon and already the tiny air conditioner was working hard to cool the beach-pod.

Outside, the sea and sky were indivisible, a continuous wash of blue, the point where they melded lost behind a narrow, white smudge of wind turbines, their asynchronously rotating blades reflecting the sun in random flashes of light.

To left and right, other pods raked tier on tier, formed a stairway down to where a slow swell slapped thickly against rusting stanchions.

Here, the sea's edge was grey and glutinous, the original sand and shingle lost long ago to the advancing waters but, for now, the southern hills had slowed their progress, the long slope of the chalk forming a new strand above the old coastal plain.

Today, the movement of the waves along the shore was slowed by a sludge of debris, the rise and fall dampened by a thin layer of microplastic and larger waste; further out, an oily sheen painted the surface an ugly green, purple and mauve.

The rising seas had crowded the population onto higher ground. Cities around the globe had filled and overflowed. New building had swallowed countryside. Waves of refugees from drowned

Seascape

lands had brought intolerable pressures to urban living. And yet, even as mankind began a forced northerly expansion into newly habitable areas of the Earth, disease, brought about by the comingling of so many disparate peoples, took hold and provided a solution, of sorts.

In such packed environments, pandemic raged uncontrolled and millions died. By the time the virus had run its course, hugely reduced, mankind had more room but had lost the facility to deal with the ecological crisis which had brought it about. Pollution remained, ice still melted, temperatures continued to rise, even though industry shrank, air, land and sea transport dwindled away and consumerism vanished as a concept from the face of the planet.

In time, of course, the cessation of such activities might bring about improvements which would return the world to its pre-industrial purity. In time. Perhaps five-hundred years; perhaps five-thousand. And perhaps, the runaway warming was already too far advanced to halt.

In the meantime, civilisation settled down to a slower pace of life. It had not returned to the Stone Age. Infrastructures held steady; power stations still ran; technology still enabled a comfortable enough style of living, albeit one which it required some decades to rebalance. Eventually, an equilibrium was achieved and people found a new way to live in an altered world.

The beach pods were a part of a freshy discovered leisure-time. A reimagining of the Victorian seaside holiday.

Five dimensional dreams

At what were once temperate latitudes, summer sunshine required serious protective measures but the lure of the edge-lands, where you could turn your back on daily life and contemplate the empty, open expanse of the ocean and the firmament was as appealing as it had ever been.

Fedra put on her polarised glasses and squinted out towards the sparkling horizon. With the unaided eye she could just make out the slowly churning sweeps of the wind turbines. From her vantage point they seemed too close to avoid each other's blades. Once, there had been fear of bird-strikes; concern for endangered wildlife; but this far south the oil and plastic had brought both food source and its avian predator to extinction and the skies were left now to the winds and the scorching sun.

She let her gaze move down to the nearer waves and along the grubby shoreline, where something lighter among the drifting flotsam seemed to move more quickly through the turgid waters. She pulled off the glasses, shaded her eyes and looked again.

There *was* something. An old container caught in an eddy maybe? As she watched, the shape dipped below the surface and rose a metre further along, pulled she guessed by the tug of some submerged netting as the currents tried to move the unyielding soup of detritus.

Then the object was gone again and again it resurfaced at a different spot. There was the suggestion too of a shadowy presence below, of a

Seascape

sinuous body, and with that thought the shape became a head.

It wasn't possible! Nothing had lived in these seas for half a century. Fedra threw back the dark-tinted shutters and climbed unsteadily to her feet. You entered the pods from the back, after climbing a metal stairway to the numbered door. The space within was just two-and-a-half metres long by one wide and was filled by an adjustable bed which moved under Fedra's feet as she came erect.

With the shutters open, the full strength of the sun striking her body was like a physical blow. She refitted the glasses and looked down the steep incline of the pods' support structure.

It was there because access to the pseudo beach was forbidden. Some of the items adrift in the filthy waves were toxic. Researchers who had collected samples had died and now the new authority which oversaw the land had forbidden entry.

The pale shape was still there, no more than a few metres from the gantry's base. From the open pod she had a clearer view. As she watched, what might have been a limb or a fin or a tail, moved lazily over the head and back into the waves.

Fedra stepped forward excitedly. There was a way down the outside of the structure if she took care. She lowered herself cautiously from the pod's rim until her left foot touched a cross-support and then she swung her body round and grasped the big diagonal stay which ran to the base. Once sitting on it, she was able to use the cross-bars as a ladder and progress downwards

Five dimensional dreams

until she was less than a metre above the ocean's scum.

The head had disappeared. She scanned the water looking for some sign of movement.

A seal? A porpoise? As a student, she'd studied the extinct marine life of these seas and it didn't seem credible. Creatures much further down the food chain had succumbed to the poisonous human waste which encircled the planet's oceans.

Someone carrying out scientific research then? She supposed that, with adequate protection, it would be possible to swim here; but to what end? The waters seemed beyond cleansing.

A voice brought her back to the moment: an urgent call from the structure above her. She turned her head, awkwardly, and squinted up across the pods to where the reflected sunlight silhouetted a waving figure.

'Get back up here! That water's dangerous!' The warning cry was reduced to a whisper by the gusting wind.

Fedra raised an arm in vague acknowledgement. It was true; she was being foolish. There could be nothing here but a curious amalgam of sodden garbage and congealed slime, forming some ridiculous semblance of life.

She was about to turn away when some movement of opposing currents drew the waters apart and formed, for a second, a still trough among the slow chop of the waves. Within it, barely submerged, was a human form; human, and yet not so; the body skeletal, the hands impossibly long-fingered, the head disproportionately large,

Seascape

with vast, black eyes clouded and sightless. It sank away even as she stared; became only the suggestion of the thing she thought she had seen, so that within moments both it and her mind's interpretation of it, were lost beneath a filthy skein of foam.

Fedra stood, desolate, searching for a second glimpse and, as she did so, she heard the same urgent voice as before, only this time much closer.

'Move back, the sea's toxic. You'll get poisoned or burned or infected – or all three!'

She felt for the rail and repositioned herself awkwardly, to face inshore. The man had followed her down the structure and was just metres away; one hand gripping the framework, the other reaching forward, fingers spread.

'Here, grab my hand.'

'There's someone in the water,' she shouted, looking back anxiously at the seething ocean. 'Or some*thing*,' she added more quietly as the man took her arm and pulled her back onto the main structure. 'It looked...alien. Big eyes, long, bony fingers.'

'It'll be the corpse of some animal that's fallen in and succumbed to the pollution. Decomposition does strange things to the flesh and the internal organs.'

'Maybe,' Fedra, shook off his hold and followed him back up towards the pod.

'My grandfather worked in coastal erosion way back,' said the man more conversationally, as they climbed. 'He used to see all sorts of stuff; he said that some of the cetaceans looked like sea

Five dimensional dreams

monsters when their skin pealed and bleached and exposed their guts. His stories used to give me the willies! Here, that's your pod; get back in and make sure you stay there. If you see anything you want to report, see me back at the kiosk.'

He waited, while Fedra re-entered her pod, and then disappeared through a service door nearby. She knelt on the sunbed but left the shutters raised and looked back, down to the ocean. From this height, the waters looked cleaner, less greasy.

An alien. As soon as she had used the word, she had felt foolish. A rotted carcass was the most plausible explanation, and yet... the thought of some extra-terrestrial visitor arriving on the Earth after eons of travel and then perishing as a result of man's stewardship of the planet, was something which, if only a flight of fancy, had brought on a very real feeling of despair and regret. How *could* they explain to such a being, how greed and complacency and a primitive and selfish drive for individual superiority had prevented co-operation and understanding and led to the slow erosion of the environment upon which they all depended. It was, as someone had once said, illogical.

She remembered an account of the inhabitants of Easter Island who, over one thousand kilometres from the nearest inhabited island and three-and-a-half thousand from the mainland, were believed to have denuded their island of trees, leaving themselves without the means to build boats and escape their self-imposed isolation.

Well, here they were: homo sapiens. Once, bound for the stars, now prisoners of their own

Seascape

island Earth - stripped bare, polluted and drowned. A millennium, if they were lucky, before they might undo the damage and contemplate such adventures again. Too red-faced to meet any roving alien and share in a cosmic confederacy. By now, she extemporised, the rest of the crew had thrown a memorial wreath into the glutinous ocean, had pulled up the ladder and taken off for other worlds, where the welcome was less...corrosive.

She sat back and pressed the control to lower the filters. The aircon purred into life as the contacts closed. She would need to be careful. She had spent too much time in the sun. She lay back and closed her eyes.

Below, the thick, tidal slew sucked and dragged at its encumbrances and another pair of eyes, huge, and cloudy-black, stared sightlessly up towards the empty sky.

The doctor will see you – now?

#1 2022

'Peter? Are you there, dear? I'm having trouble with this telephone.'

'What sort of trouble? If it's one of those nuisance calls - I've told you before - just hang up. '

'No, it's not that. I'm trying to phone Dr Hargreaves and I've got a recorded message.'

'Not surprised. Dr Hargreaves died about twenty years ago.'

'Don't be facetious dear. You know what I mean. I call him that because I can't remember the new doctor's name. It's foreign.'

'That's because *he's* foreign, Mother. Look, what is the message telling you to do?'

'It said, if I was suffering from a life-threatening condition, I should replace the receiver and call nine, nine, nine.'

'And are you? Suffering from a life-threatening condition?'

'No, of course not! I just want to speak to him about my blood pressure pills; they don't agree with me.'

'Well, what else are they saying?'

'Right now, they're telling me about the coronavirus infection. I haven't got coronavirus.'

'Keep listening.'

'I am, listening...oh dear!'

The doctor will see you…now?

'What?'

'All the lines are busy and I should call back…'

'Well, they might have told you that to begin with!'

'…and do I know about their new online questionnaire? It could save me hanging on the phone in future.'

'Ah, yes; I've heard about that. You fill in all your symptoms and the doctor calls you back and tells you what he thinks is the trouble.'

'I know what the trouble is, dear. The tablets are keeping me awake at night.'

'Well, then - he'll prescribe a different medication. Come on, hang up; we'll give it a try.'

#2 2022

"Please speak slowly and clearly. Give your name and your NHS Number when you hear the tone. Then answer each of the questions which the Healthy U Hub asks you. If you are unsure about how to proceed or you feel concerned at any time, just say, 'Stop please,' and wait for a member of the health centre staff to answer your call."

Beep.

'Oh, ah, hello, er, I'm Peter Frond. My NHS number is ZP674238. I'm calling on behalf of…'

"Please state the reason for your call. Use no more than four words. For example, you might say, I have a headache; I have been sick; My back aches. Please speak after the tone."

Five dimensional dreams

Beep.
'Ah, well, *I'm* not actually unwell. I'm calling about my mother, Mrs Iris Frond. She filled in an online form a couple of months ago...'
"Error. You have used more than four words. Please state the reason for your call. Use no more than four words. For example, you might say, I have a headache; I have been sick; My back aches. Please speak after the tone."

Beep.
Good grief, – 'Wrong, tablets.'
"You have the wrong tablets. Please say 'Yes' if this is correct. Please speak after the tone."

Beep.
Oh, for heaven's – 'Yes.'
'Which tablets do you have? Please speak after the tone."

Beep.
'Er, they're called – mm, let's see. Hold on, I need my glasses for this...'
"I am unable to identify that medication. Please repeat the name of the tablets. Please speak after the tone."

Beep
'Aphromedic – they're Aphromedic.'
"The tablets are called 'Aphromedic'. Please say 'yes' if this is correct. Please speak after the tone."

Beep.
'YES!'
"Please speak in a normal tone. The Healthy U Hub may not respond if you do not speak slowly and clearly. Say 'Yes' if you understand. Please speak after the tone."

The doctor will see you...now?

Beep.
'Forget it! I'll try Google. Goodbye.'
"If you do not respond within ten seconds this call will be terminated. Please confirm you wish to terminate the call by answering 'Yes' after the tone."
Beep.

#3 2030

'Good morning, my name is Peter Frond. My NHS number is ZP674238. I am calling about my recent blood test.'
"Good morning Mr Frond. Thank you for calling Depudoc UK. I have the results of your blood test and these are available to download to your smartphone. Would you like a summary of the results?"
'Yes please.'
"I will have these sent to you using our secure online link. You will require your personal, Depudoc UK Pin Number to access them. Can I help you with anything else this morning?"
'Well, yes, you see I've been getting this shooting pain when I bend over or lift anything. Right across my lower back.'
"It sounds like you need to see the doctor. I can arrange an appointment. The earliest will be Wednesday, September 12 at 9.30am."
'September 12? But it's only May 10!'
"You are not obliged to accept this appointment but you are strongly advised to do so as the health

Five dimensional dreams

centre is experiencing an increased demand for services. Are you aware that we now operate an automated service which may be able to identify your problem and offer assistance?"

'But aren't I speaking to it?'

'Just call this number and ask for Depudoc UK. Thank you for your enquiry. Goodbye."

#4 2040

"Good morning Mr Frond! Thank you for calling Condichek 2030, the very latest AI remote diagnostic service brought to you by FixoPharm, the world's largest manufacturer of pharmaceuticals, working in collaboration with your National Health Service. Please call me, Doctor Fine! I see from your ID that you have been a customer at this practice for quite a time now."

'Yes, that's right Doctor, er, Fine, my late mother was a patient of Doctor Hargreaves way back.'

"Ah, Doctor Hargreaves MB BS MA Oxon MRCGP DRCOG DFFP, 2002 to 2021: an excellent physician!"

'You're very well informed, Doctor.'

"The FixoPharm database is the most comprehensive of its kind, Mr Frond. I can see for example that the late Mrs Frond's last action was to complete an online questionnaire in June, 2020 regarding her medication for hypertension - although, oddly, the results of that enquiry do not

The doctor will see you...now?

seem to have been logged. I trust that the outcome was satisfactory?"

'Sadly, she died before she received a response. Heart attack.'

"Well, of course Doctor Hargreaves worked without the advantage of modern diagnostics, like the FixoPharm BioBot 600. Now, how can I assist you this morning Mr Frond – or may I call you Peter?"

'Mr Frond will do fine, Fine. Anyway, I'm seventy-five today and I understand I qualify for a free medical check-up under the new government guidelines.'

"That's correct Mr Frond. Let's begin, shall we? I take it you have your personal FixoPharm BioBot 600 to hand? BioBot, BioBot - know what's what with BioBot! I'm sure you're familiar with the jingle! That's right, just insert your hand into the sleeve and relax."

'How long will this take Doctor...*Fine?*'

"All done, Mr Frond! The advanced algorithms utilised by the BioBot 600 can perform twenty-five different tests in five seconds! Isn't that incredible?"

'Incredible. Well, come on, what's the analysis of all that mumbo-jumbo? Do you expect me to live to be a hundred and ten?'

"No Mr Frond, I expect you to die! Ha ha! Just my little joke Mr Frond. The Condichek 2030 is programmed to interact with clients in a relaxed and friendly manner. If you would rather I adopted a more formal response pattern, just say,

Five dimensional dreams

'Can it, Fine'. The software can adapt to every client's preferences."
'Can it, Fine.'
"It certainly can! Ho ho! Got you there, Frond! They fall for it every time! Let's see, bloodpressure120over80;HDLCholesterol1.5;LDL2;Non 2; HDL4liverfunctiondandedahheartrythmmmandson andsoonetcetc......Mmm, nothing much to worry about there. Perhaps a touch of...and maybe...but then, for your age...I wouldn't be too concerned Mr Frond. I'm pretty sure you'll still be able to play the piano! You can remove your hand from the BioBot 600 by the way. Give me a call in six months' time. Next please!"

#5 2060

"Welcome to the OurLife Clinic Mr Frond. Please sit in the comfort booth, secure the lap restraint and watch the pink screen. The InterMed is scanning your bodily functions and analysing your genomic stability, telomere attrition rates and epigenetic alteration. You may feel a slight tingling sensation as the nano-probs enter the pore-openings at the base of your skull; this is perfectly normal. Do you have any questions at this stage of the procedure, Mr Frond?"
'Well, yes, I was wondering why I'd been called to the clinic in the first place. I haven't needed to contact my Health Control Centre for a while now. In fact, I'm feeling pretty good considering my age.'

The doctor will see you...now?

"It is government policy to review the life viability of all citizens at age ninety-five."

'You mean you're going to calculate how long I've got left? I'm not so sure I want to know that. At my age, you tend to live life on a day-by-day basis. You know - if you wake up in the morning, you know you're still alive!'

"The purpose of your visit is not to ascertain *life expectancy Mr Frond. Rather it is to* determine *it."*

'Sorry?'

"The current population of the UK is seventy-five million. This is considered unsustainable."

'How does that concern me?'

"Just sit back and relax Mr Frond; the nano probs will infuse a medication which will assist this process. Please begin to count down from ten."

'Well, I suppose... ten, nine, eight seven, siiiiiiii....................'

Uptight

'Bloody Hodgson.' Farthingright reached into the containment chamber and withdrew the test subject from the beam target. On one side, paired indentations marked the area where a large segment of flesh had been removed.

He had personally taken responsibility for setting-up the experiment and knew for sure that the apple had been intact at that point. It was only a dozen metres to the shielded firing zone and so Hodgson - for surely it *was* Hodgson - must have waited his chance and snatched the fruit, bitten into it and returned it to the chamber, all within seconds of the quantum trigger being activated.

It was all so bloody childish, and just the sort of thing that the project's senior maths graduate would find unaccountably amusing.

The trouble was, Farthingright acknowledged, if only to himself, Hodgson was a totally brilliant scientist and could probably dance naked on the dean's lawn without endangering his sinecure at the university's research facility.

If Farthingright was honest with himself, the young man had annoyed him from the outset, from the moment he was thrust upon his team.

'He's an amazing acquisition,' the chancellor had insisted, when Farthingright had protested at the imposition. 'Quite outstanding. He was eyeing up Stanford before he heard about your group. Jumped at the chance. His special field of interest

Uptight

apparently. You and he could achieve big things, Farthingright.'

And Farthingright had rejoined that he was expecting to achieve big things anyway, with or without the assistance of some bright-eyed young upstart – only he hadn't put it quite that way and, in the eventuality, Hodgson had proved invaluable in cracking the more obstinate problems associated with matter transference, and Farthingright's displeasure had been tempered if not entirely dispelled.

The trouble was that Hodgson didn't seem to take any of their work seriously. That was to say, he toiled diligently at the thorny aspects of their research and found solutions to seemingly insoluble difficulties; had in fact, in no small way, enabled the project to be brought to fruition, but he had acted throughout like an irksome schoolboy; playing pranks on other team members; loading his presentations with innuendo; interfering, in the most juvenile fashion, with serious experimentation. The apple was simply the latest example of his immaturity.

Farthingright had found that remonstrating with Hodgson had little effect. He would express contrition and smile an apology and within hours, there would be yet another demonstration of his infantile mindset.

So, such confrontations seemed pointless - and yet, on this occasion, Farthingright felt an obligation to bring his wayward assistant to heel.

'Look here, Hodgson,' he began, when the other answered his summons and was lounging

Five dimensional dreams

disrespectfully across from his desk, 'what the hell do you think you were playing at with that apple. Supposing you'd got your hand in the way of the transfer beam when the trigger was released. There's no knowing what might have happened.'

'Have you seen The Fly?' asked Hodgson, incongruously. 'Bluebottle gets into the containment space and the first human guinea-pig ends up with multi-faceted eyes and antennae! I suppose something like that might have happened to me if I hadn't been quick. You'd have found my neatly severed hand holding the apple in the receiver. Quite a shock, eh! I wonder if the action would have cauterised the wound?'

Farthingright stared at his co-worker, nonplussed, and struggled for a moment to identify the reference. It was just the sort of non-sequitur which Hodgson employed to divert attention from his behaviour; and that seemingly trivial addendum about the injury would be no such thing either. Within the hour Hodgson was likely to provide chapter and verse on the subject with carefully reasoned propositions and a suggested program of research. It was, Farthingright admitted reluctantly, a perfect illustration of the chancellor's proposition – that the younger man was an extraordinary asset to both the project in particular and to the university in general.

'Don't you consider the possible consequences of your actions?' he asked, despairingly. 'Do you suppose that losing a hand would be helpful to your future career? And besides,' he hurried on, before the other could respond, 'the implications to

Uptight

our research would be considerable. I imagine there'd be an enquiry, with all current work suspended during the investigation. Months of wrangling with the Health & Safety brigade. All manner of inconvenience. Your actions were ill-considered Hodgson, to say the least.'

'Oh, for Christ's sake, Farthingright!'

Hodgson's response was so unexpectedly vehement that Farthingright actually sat back, as if from a physical blow.

'Swopping those damned apples took a second at most. I don't imagine I was in much danger of bringing your whole effing edifice tumbling down about your ears, was I?'

Farthingright was too taken aback to reply. On previous occasions when he had found it necessary to reprimand his junior colleague, the response had always been one of self-reproach and regret. Until this moment, he had taken it for granted that such wayward conduct reflected a guileless nature; or a lack of sophistication which more mature social contact would, eventually, instruct. Now, the revelation came to him that it was in fact an intentional act of rebellion; a reaction to Farthingright's own more formal and, in Hodgson's eye's, restrictive, codes of practice.

He raised his chin in defiance of such a possibility.

'Don't you think you owe me a certain respect - as head of department?'

Hodgson pursed his lips as if to indicate that he was giving the question due consideration. 'Well,' he said, after an instructive pause, 'I think you're a

Five dimensional dreams

top-class physicist. And your work here is cutting edge. It's the reason I agreed to join the team.'

Farthingright grunted a response, intended to indicate an embarrassed acceptance of the observation, whilst noting too, that his question had not been answered. Science was a serious business, wasn't it? Was there room for levity? For, at least, a kind of exuberance? In short, did he need to lighten-up? Find the exhilaration which had taken him into a field which many had seen at best as highly speculative and a few as no more than pseudo-scientific.

Once, he realised, he himself had been far from conventional. Oh, not as frivolous and irreverent as Hodgson; but a maverick, for sure: someone who was unwilling to toe the line for the sake of appearances. The approach had been different; the aim - to disassociate himself from blinkered conformity - somewhat similar.

'But did you need to resort to the nonsense of the apple?' he said, vocalising his train of thought but scarcely addressing it to anywhere other than his own musings. 'I mean, what was it all *about?*'

'It was just a joke,' responded Hodgson. He sounded weary of the whole thing and his voice had lost its accusatory tone. 'I thought it would make you grin, when you saw the switch, maybe.'

Farthingright looked up, a new thought tracing through his mind. Was it conceivable that the young man had not set out to antagonise him at all, but simply to...engage with him? And what if he *had* laughed? Would it have been so terrible a thing?

Uptight

He allowed his face to relax into a facsimile of a smile. 'It was, amusing, I suppose,' he said awkwardly and with as much warmth as he could generate, this early in their new relationship. Then another thought struck him. 'You've mentioned an exchange of apples more than once. What do you mean?'

Hodgson looked askance at his superior. 'Why, isn't that what this is all about?' he said. 'Turning your Golden Delicious into an Egremont Russett? I did wonder if you'd notice - you're always so wrapped up in the science - but then I thought, even you could scarcely fail to notice if one variety left the transmitter and an altogether different one arrived at the receiver.'

The smile achieved with such emotional self-sacrifice faded on Farthingright's face. The original fruit had been glossy green. He pictured the subject of all his anguish: a pale, matt brown.

'No, Paul,' he said, 'I didn't notice. I thought it was the bite you'd taken out of the apple which was the intended joke.'

Hodgson, thoroughly distracted by the use of his first name, took a moment to frame a reply. 'Oh, that,' he managed at last. 'I'd forgotten about that.'

'Forgotten?' Farthingright could feel his new spirit of bonhomie evaporating before it had fully coalesced. 'What the hell does that mean?'

Hodgson looked discomfited. 'Well, I was monitoring the receiver, remember? When the damned apple appeared, I took a bite – just to check it was as it should be, sort of thing.'

'And then put it back in the chamber for me to

Five dimensional dreams

find.'

'Yes, I suppose so – although I hadn't thought about it to be honest. It never occurred to me that you'd be mad about it. I mean, it *was* only an apple. It was the act of transfer that was important. Not the subject. And anyway...I was hungry.'

Farthingright opened his mouth to reply but for the second time during their conversation found himself lost for an immediate response. Maybe that was right; it *was* only an apple and it had merely re-affirmed the principles of macro-matter transference. The breakthrough had been a week ago and the euphoria generated by that first success had abated as further tests had been conducted. Perhaps there *was* room for a little relaxation. He felt an inner satisfaction at the thought.

Uptight Farthingright. Yes, he'd heard the whispered mockery. Well, no more! He realised Hodgson was speaking to him and brought his thoughts back to the present.

'Sorry?'

'I said, is that all you wanted? Can I go now?'

Farthingright stiffened at the tone of the request. He almost expected Hodgson to add a sarcastic, "Sir" to the question. *Yes, yes, you can run along, Hodgson*, was the answer which suggested itself, but he resisted its delivery. Was this how his co-workers perceived him: as some kind of authoritarian throwback? The thought disturbed him but was suddenly over-ridden by another, more urgent consideration.

Uptight

'No, there is one more thing, Hodgson,' he said with sudden forcefulness. 'If you replaced the original apple with your own, perhaps you'd like to explain exactly what has happened to my Golden Delicious?

Divergence 4: end game

Gregory was pretty sure he was the last person on Earth. He had no way to confirm the belief and nothing to gain from doing so, but given his age, it seemed more than likely.

The radio had been silent on every frequency for decades now and he could no longer recall when he had last glimpsed another human being. Sometime in '80 maybe, when he had made his final foray down into the city and loaded a truck with enough canned food to see him through to the end.

He'd imagined at the time that another ten years would see him out but despite his privations, or maybe because of them, he had lived on and by his calculations would be one-hundred-and-five this winter.

The cold would probably have done for him this time around. He'd barely survived the previous snowfalls and the long, dark months confined to the house had been difficult ones. The generator still ran, powered by the ceaseless flow of the river, and so he had power for lights and tools and, increasingly, for evenings listening to music on the old hi-fi.

He'd been lucky up until now. Genetically equipped for a healthy life – that was what he would have told people. No arthritis, no dementia; for his age he was in damn good condition - had been, at any rate.

End game

Over the years there had been one or two difficult moments. A tooth abscess, somewhere in his forties; that had been nasty for a week or so. He'd had a cupboardful of antibiotics and even some novocaine, acquired from a downtown dentist's stores; but he'd had trouble finding the courage to use the syringe, afraid that the needle would break in his trembling hands. When he'd finally managed it, he'd extracted the tooth using tools from the same abandoned clinic. It had been messy and painful and, in the absence of stitching, he'd had to press wads of cotton wool into his gum to stop the bleeding; but he still remembered the relief and the joy of an undisturbed night's sleep and the satisfaction of having brought himself through the crisis.

There had been other things: a broken finger; cracked ribs; and his eyesight had deteriorated so that he could no longer see the stars as he once had. But these were small concerns over such an extended lifetime and he had begun to feel that the end might be just as uneventful. A quiet descent into endless sleep.

He'd been twelve when the virus came and still only in his teens when it had claimed the lives of his parents and several billion of the global population. A few months in, scientists had discovered that the virus attacked the reproductive capacity of both men and women and the significant thing suddenly became not the number of deaths but the number of people infected. By then treatment had proved to be more effective than vaccination and a degree of complacency had

Five dimensional dreams

crept in. Allowing the virus to spread had been seen as a sensible procedure, given that the worst of the symptoms could be easily supressed and, as parents had once encouraged their children to catch chickenpox to gain future immunity, governments relaxed all restrictions in the hope that their citizens would do the same.

The understanding that this might also render them sterile had come too late to prevent disaster. When the virus mutated into a new and even more infectious strain, resistant to vaccination, the die had been cast.

Like everyone else, Gregory had succumbed to the disease, responded quickly to treatment and, when tested, had found himself infertile.

After that, it had been just a matter of watching the human race fade away.

To begin with, life went on as before. Trade and industry faltered, were tentatively re-established and then dwindled again as the pointlessness of such activities became apparent. Free of responsibility to future generations, Earth's current custodians increasingly adopted a hedonistic and yet languid lifestyle; pursuing pleasure without passion; distraction without gratification.

Slowly society unravelled. Businesses closed; services withdrew. For a while a mild anarchy took hold: shops were looted, cars stolen, properties annexed, but in the end, finding that they had nothing against which to rail, even the lawless and the wayward lost their fervour.

End game

At some point Gregory had left it all behind; driven into the hills, found an empty house and set about making it his fortress and his haven. He had always been good with machinery and the generator he hauled from a nearby engineering works quickly reinstated the electricity supply. Food he collected from a deserted supermarket, although it had already been raided and on his third visit, he found it empty. Requisitioning a truck, he had made his way to an out-of-town warehouse and loaded aboard all he could carry. Then he had found a storage facility, acquired the keys to a container from the empty office and locked his plunder securely away. He had repeated this procedure until the warehouse was denuded of supplies and he possessed food enough for decades of single meals. And he had found seed and grown vegetables to supplement his canned diet. It was only later that he confessed to himself that his efforts to provide for his survival were themselves, looting, of a sort. The difference being that, by now, the stores and warehouses which he visited were ownerless, with no one to claim possession.

For some time too, he made occasional contact with other survivors; people who like him had found sanctuary in the countryside around the decaying city. He encountered them on expeditions for supplies or on hikes through the hills. For a year or two there had been a relationship with a woman in the next valley. Now and again, he would trek over to see her and they conducted a desultory love affair which lasted until one day he made the journey and found her house was empty,

Five dimensional dreams

her belongings gone. She had left no note and he had no notion of her reasons to depart, other than commitment had never been a part of their agenda.

By the time he was sixty, the hills were empty, the dusty roads deserted, the city an echoing ruin, populated only by feral creatures.

He reckoned time as running from the year his mother died, and he imagined a child born then who was perhaps the last of his kind. Gregory had been fifteen and so by now the child would be ninety. They might still be out there somewhere, but life was hard and accident and illness and a lack of medical services meant few would have lived into advanced old age. By now, he accepted he was alone, or as near as made little difference, and when he died, so would his species. A hundred-thousand years of existence ended with his last breath. Not so long when you thought of the dinosaurs and their one-hundred-and-eighty-million-year reign.

And yet he had seen himself as the one who had won through; held the ground on behalf of the human race. Survived against the odds.

Which made dying of the virus all the more wretched.

It was passed from person to person, that he had always known. Keep your distance and you were safe; and the eradication of every other member of homo sapiens should have precluded this eventuality. So, it was the damn squirrel which he'd pulled from a trap a fortnight earlier and

End game

skinned and cooked and enjoyed. The first fresh meat he'd seen in months.

The whole thing, he'd read, had started with food taken from the wild and now, a century later, he had repeated the mistake and the virus had won after all.

With an effort, Gregory raised his slender frame from the bed and looked towards the open sky beyond his window. The world was a beautiful place and it would continue to be so. Some other creature would rise to dominance, or maybe not. Perhaps the Earth would find a balance at last and life would simply persist until the sun went bang and there was nothing left but the stars.

He fell back onto the pillow, retching dryly; gasping for breath until his final breath had been taken and he was no longer the last man on Earth.

Time and Punishment

I didn't set out to murder Hitler, you understand. As I left Oxford on that sunny morning, I had no idea that within minutes I would encounter the evil megalomaniac who had brought chaos and death to such unprecedented numbers of people all across the globe; but when I found myself staring into those cold, blue eyes, I didn't feel a moment's hesitation; I gave no consideration to the consequences of my actions and I felt nothing but satisfaction as I watched his body tumble down the rocky bank into the path of the oncoming truck. I felt sure that, whatever world I returned to, it would be one which had arisen from a cleaner, less traumatised age than the one which my parents had known.

'Ah, Professor Thomson, welcome back to 2025.'

I peered up groggily, from my bed, blinked to clear my vision and pushed myself slowly into a sitting position.

The man who had spoken occupied the armchair in the corner of the room, near to the desk.

'And who, are you?' I asked, reaching behind me and adjusting the pillows. It was an action which had more to do with buying time for his appraisal than improving my comfort; I hadn't expected company on my return. In fact, as far as I knew, there was no other living soul who was aware of the journey I had so recently undertaken.

Time and punishment

And there was another reason to be surprised by my unexpected visitor: the interval between my departure and the moment of reawakening to the sound of his voice, had been brief to say the least; in fact, in a very real sense, no time at all had passed since I had imbibed that witch's brew of chemicals and nano-particles, even though I had spent the best part of an hour at a location more than 800 miles from my accommodation, here in the university.

I swung my feet around and lowered them to the floor; I still felt a little detached from reality but I managed to stand and took a few unsteady steps across the room to a chair, onto which I lowered myself before shuffling round to face my uninvited guest.

The first impression was of a man dressed for a funeral: heavy black coat, black suit, stout black shoes. He might have been a pallbearer or the undertaker himself and for a surreal moment I wondered if my unconscious body had been perceived as dead and someone had summoned his services. But a dark crimson flash across his black tie belied that suggestion and in further counterpoint to the sombre garb, his square-jawed face and piercing blue eyes were complimented by pale, cropped hair.

'Who are you?' I repeated, this time with more belligerence.

He inclined his head a little and a half-smile formed across his angular countenance.

'You might think of me as someone with a lifetime's interest in T, B, E,' he said, pronouncing

Five dimensional dreams

each of those final three letters with a determined precision.

He spoke in a quietly controlled manner and yet his words hit me like a tsunami. I gaped back, became aware I was doing so and shut my mouth slowly.

'What do you know of Temporal Bio-entanglement?' I asked, when I had recovered my composure sufficiently to frame the question.

He smiled again, but this time there was a hint of something less pleasant in his expression. 'Oh, I know a great deal about your activities Professor. I've shown an interest in your career from the very start and although I cannot claim to understand the technicalities of your work I have, with some help from others, been able to unravel a little of the mysteries of your quantum world.'

I shook my head vigorously. 'That's not possible. There's no one else in the field. I invented the damned term for God's sake. And anyway, you couldn't possibly have studied my notes, leave alone consulted with others – not in the time I've been ...unconscious.'

He nodded. The smile was gone now, replaced by a stare of such intensity that I was quelled into silence once more.

'No, of course not. Not in those few moments that you were absent from your body.

'Quantum entanglement is a curious, even bizarre concept which involves the measurement of one particle affecting the state of another entangled particle, even though the two may be separated by vast distance.' He looked at me for assurance and I

Time and punishment

gave it with a nod.

'I admit, he said, 'that I still find that a, "Lewis Carroll" notion, and my advisors have been unable to bring me to a full understanding of *"entanglement"* but, be that as it may, I know that science accepts the theory as proven.

'So, your research found a temporal aspect to this strange arrangement; that the same effect pertained not only across space but across time as well.'

My enthusiasm for my field overcame my reticence and I took up the point. 'That's right! To put it crudely, under certain circumstances one of those particles observed today will alter the state of the other next week – or last week – or at any time that the two particles exist!'

This time it was the man who nodded before returning to his exposition. 'Let us cut to the chase, Professor Thomson. You discovered a biological component to all this which led you to conceive of a form of time travel. No,' he saw me about to interrupt again, and held up a hand to stop me. 'My grasp of the method may be incomplete and it is most certainly unscientific but the fact of the matter is this. You developed a way to link your consciousness to that of another person living at a different point in time and, in that way, were able to observe his world. Is this not so?'

'Yes, yes, but not just any person; there needs to be an inherited biological element. An imbedded memory trace, shared by both parties. In other words, to establish such a partnership you must meld with a genetically similar mind; an individual

Five dimensional dreams

who is you own ancestor.'

'Or, perhaps, your own descendant?' He waved that thought aside, 'but that is for another time,' he smirked, to show that the pun was intentional. 'Tell me of your most recent trial and please, do not prevaricate, I know too much of your story for that tactic to succeed.'

This last directive was enunciated so commandingly that I decided there and then to narrate the tale in its entirety. After all, I had nothing to regret in my actions even if the world to which I had returned could not be fully aware of their consequences.

'You can, to some degree, tune the cocktail of drugs that induces the transference,' I began, 'and so I had a good idea of just how far back I might find myself and just whose body I'd find myself in.'

'My parents were Germans who got out of the country in '38, when they saw which way the wind was blowing. They didn't need to leave you understand, they simply didn't want to be a part of what was going on. It caused a permanent division in the family because my paternal grandfather was a member of the party and considered their actions were close to treason. I tell you this to explain why I had chosen my grandfather as a target: I'd never met him and I was intrigued to find out what made him tick. It was a trifle self-indulgent I suppose, but as a first test for TBA, he seemed ideal.

'I prepared the drugs, lay down on the bed and waited. I had no concern for being discovered because I knew that when the effects wore off, I'd return to the precise second of the Twenty-First

Time and punishment

century which I had left. At the time, the interval between then and now didn't seem all that relevant. I see now that I was perhaps mistaken.

'Anyway, almost straight away I felt myself slipping into unconsciousness; then there was a brief period of nausea and I opened my eyes on an extraordinary sight.

'I say, "opened *my* eyes," but of course, they weren't mine, they were my grandfather's and they were already open before I rose to awareness within his mind.

'He was standing on a wide, sloping driveway. The ground fell away before him revealing a view of high, pine-covered hills and towering mountain peaks, their snowy summits reflecting the bright sunshine. On the drive a car stood, the driver at attention and holding the door for a uniformed officer who had already alighted and was striding towards us, a broad smile on his face.

'The car's pennant and the officer's uniform left no doubt as to their allegiance: the familiar red and white insignia with the cruel, angular shape of the swastika at its centre.

' "Herwig. Es ist schön, dich wiederzusehen. Führt der Küchenchef immer noch seinen Zauber mit dem lokalen Wildschwein aus?"

'I knew little German but in a way which is difficult to explain, my Grandfather's understanding of the words became clear to me through his brain's translation of them into visual images and emotional responses. At any rate, it was obvious that my predecessor was well liked, at least by this member of the SS.

Five dimensional dreams

'Grandfather responded. "Willkommen noch einmal zum Berghof, Oberstgruppenführer, Lass mich deine Tasche tragen," or, as I understood it to be, "Welcome to the Berghof, Oberstgruppenführer, let me carry your bag."

'I confess that in the new confusion brought about at my extraordinary circumstances, the reference to the "Berghof" failed to register.

'We turned and walked towards a building that drew comparison with an Alpine hotel. My grandfather marched up to it, threw open a door and waved the officer inside. Then, as we proceeded down a long corridor, he explained the location and time of a meeting which was to take place later that morning. At a particular spot he stopped, opened a second door and we entered what was obviously the officer's accommodation for the duration of his stay.

'All this while I had been a silent observer: but I was curious about the limits of my influence over my host and without thinking I turned his head to take in the view from the picture window. It was a mistake. He cried out and clasped his neck and the SS man swung round in concern and enquired as to his problem.

' "It's nothing Oberstgruppenführer, merely a muscle spasm. I fear I grow older by the day. My apologies for my ill-mannered response."

'The officer tut-tutted his sympathy and after a few more re-assurances as to his health my Grandfather hurried away.

'Once in the corridor again, he stopped at a window and examined his reflection, twisting his

Time and punishment

head cautiously to left and right. It provided me with my first opportunity to see him. A swarthy man with a military bearing and a prominent scar on his right cheek. He was in the act of further exercises when a telephone rang and he crossed the floor, opened a wall-mounted box and lifted a receiver. The conversation was short and in the form of an urgent instruction but more than that I was unable to decipher. My Grandfather reacted by brushing down his uniform, adjusting his tie and using both hands to smooth back his hair, then he marched briskly off back down the corridor and turned left under an archway which led out onto a wide terrace, with a central lawn and a surrounding footpath.

'On the further side of the lawn a figure sat petting a large, German Sheppard and looking out at the same panoramic view of hills and mountains which had so caught my attention earlier.

'Even then I did not guess who that man might be, although in hindsight, it seems obvious that you, listening to my tale, will have guessed at once that it was Adolf Hitler, The Fuhrer, the leader of The Third Reich and the man who had plunged so much of the world into war in 1939.

'But I had no knowledge of the role my Grandfather had played in that conflict, of where he had served or in what capacity and so, that moment, when he strode across the lawn and clicked to attention, and the face which I had seen on a thousand newsreels turned and smiled up at him, that moment was one of the most astounding in my entire life.

Five dimensional dreams

' "Ah, Herwig, it is a beautiful day is it not? Tell me, has our final guest arrived yet?"

'It was fortunate that my Grandfather was in control of the body which, for the present, we both occupied, because I was mentally dazed.

'The Berghof - of course! Hitler's eyrie in the Bavarian Alps; how could I have been so slow? And it seemed that my ancestor was a trusted member of his staff, on familiar terms with the man who, at this moment in history, was the most powerful leader in the civilised world.

'I am not prone to violence. Up until that moment I cannot recall ever having struck anyone, even as a child in a schoolyard brawl; but as I stared back into those cold, blue eyes, something inside me – or inside the consciousness which had made that amazing transfer from one entity to another: from one century to another; and which was now enmeshed within the structure of my grandfather's brain – something, impelled me to action.

'I did not know whether the man before me was truly evil or whether a kind of insanity had led him to commit the atrocities with which the world was so familiar but I knew, in that instant, that I must kill him. I knew that others had tried – or would try; the chronology was uncertain to me – and that there were many who wished to sue for peace: the professional military men who were aghast at the cruelty and barbarism of the regime they served. With Hitler dead, the way would be open for more rational minds to end the conflict and save the lives of millions. But I can't say that in that second of recognition, such an analysis was foremost in

Time and punishment

my thoughts. It was simply that a revulsion welled up within me at all he would bring about. A recollection of a hundred pictures of emaciated bodies and despairing faces; of heaped shoes and carefully written legers of death.

'Whether my grandfather could have resisted, had he been aware of my presence and my intentions, I don't know, but as it was, he offered no opposition as I took control of his body and stepped forward.

'The dog tensed and growled softly, sensing menace in my movement but Hitler only looked mildly surprised in the second before I reached down, grabbed his legs and tipped him over the parapet. The action was so unexpected that he didn't even throw out a hand, he merely fell backwards into space, his body rotating slowly as he vanished from sight.

'It was my grandfather who called out: something between a shriek of bewildered surprise and an anguished scream.

'He took another urgent step to the low wall and craned out to see the view below. To my consternation it became clear that the gardens did not stand above a mountain chasm as I had assumed but that the base of the wall, twenty feet below, rose from a gently inclined grassy bank which sloped down to a roadway, where a convoy of lorries was winding its way up to the Berghof from the valley, far below.

'As we watched, I, horrified that my attempt at assassination should be so ill conceived, he, stunned by his involuntary action, Hitler's body

Five dimensional dreams

tumbled down the bank and fell the final few feet onto the tarmac.

'Despite the fall, he was still conscious and struggled to one knee as the first vehicle, rounding a final bend in the road, struck him full force and his body disappeared beneath its wheels.

'The door to the lorry's cab was flung open, a man leapt down, shouting as he did so; my uncle wrenched control of his reluctant body and began to run towards the door from the garden; somewhere below, a whistle blew, sharp and repetitively; the dog barked furiously; there was the sound of boots echoing from the stone-floored corridors within. In short, within seconds of the vehicle's impact with Hitler's battered, crouching body, all hell broke loose.'

'What was the culmination of all this panic and disorder? I have no idea, for it was then that the effects of the drug left my system, like the last grains of sand sifting through an hour glass and in a flash, I found myself back in my bed, blinking myopically at a different day in a different time.

'So, did he die?' I asked the man sitting across from me. He didn't reply, he merely raised an eyebrow and tilted his head in a manner which seemed to say, "What do you think?" and with that unspoken question the answer suddenly formed in my mind and a whole new knowledge of my life and of my world, coalesced and imbedded itself in the very fabric of my being.

'Of *course* he died!' I cried, 'there was some sort of accident in the mountains. A fall, a car crash, it was never fully revealed. Some people believe he

Time and punishment

was the victim of an assassination...' I tailed off, aware of the implication of what I was saying.

'But the war didn't end, did it?' I continued, after a few moments' introspection.

'No,' said the man seated across from me, 'it didn't. Freed from Hitler's increasing paranoia, the generals took control and secured a famous victory. The Americans declined to interfere and The New German Republic introduced order and organisation across the European continent.'

'I know,' I said, quietly. 'I've always known, from childhood. "The benevolent Fatherland, which snatched us from the maul of the great dictator". It's the first thing we learn in intermediate education. And yet...' I added, 'I learned it just a moment ago, when I changed history and returned to find my new past.

'So, why are you here? What do you want of me? How did you find me?'

'Ah,' said the other, 'you've led me quite a chase, I can tell you! To begin with, I never believed your grandfather murdered the Fuhrer. That's the official view by the way. The investigation at the time was pretty clear that he suffered some sort of "mental seizure" and committed the act while the balance of his mind was disturbed. That conclusion was never made public because it suited the newly formed government for people to believe that he was removed by one of their "Liberation Brigade." So, they let the rumours circulate and let people write their own histories. But I was a party to the truth about what happened at the Berghof and I always had my doubts.

Five dimensional dreams

'To begin with, your grandfather had no background of mental illness and he had been screened most thoroughly before being granted a position so near to the seat of power. And then, he was known as one of the regime's most loyal supporters. The Fuhrer had known him for decades and trusted him implicitly.

'I started a new investigation...and it led to nothing. I checked out his nearest relatives of course and found out about your parents' desertion of their homeland but I couldn't see a connection with Hitler's death. In the end I put it all on hold but asked for a regular report on anyone linked to the family.'

'And eventually, that brought you to me.'

'Yes, but it didn't seem likely that you were involved in an incident which took place before you were born. Until...'

'You heard about my research into Temporal Bio-Entanglement.'

'I did, but remember, this was decades later and my interest in the matter had waned by then. Never the less I took a look at the paper you had published. At first, I dismissed it as too esoteric to be of relevance and most of it was beyond my comprehension anyway and then, one evening I found myself speaking to a science journalist who told me of the strange conclusions of a new piece of research.'

'And you began to put two and two together.'

'Yes, and I admit I became obsessed all over again. Lately I've had you watched all round the clock and yesterday, I received a report that you

Time and punishment

were planning some important experiment. Even so, it was sheer luck that I chose today to speak to you. I had intended to sound you out; ascertain your plans, but in fact I found you here, unconscious with a sheaf of notes by your bedside. They have made fascinating reading while I waited for you to regain consciousness.'

'OK, that's the how, what about the why? I suppose I'm your mysterious freedom fighter? The man behind the myth. Do you intend to use me as propaganda? How a Federation scientist saved the world.'

'Oh no, Professor Thomson. My pursuit of you as been for entirely different reasons. Perhaps I should introduce myself? I'm Ordnungspolizei Generaloberst Fischer and I am here to arrest you for the murder of the Fuhrer. I should advise you that you have been found guilty in your absence and sentence will be carried out with immediate effect. Please roll up your sleeve.'

For a moment I froze, in horror, then I grabbed for the glass next to my bed and swallowed the remaining contents in a single gulp.

The Fuhrer was still waiting, with his dog, by the low garden wall overlooking the mountains. My grandfather clicked to attention and awaited his orders, and I watched silently through his eyes, and did nothing at all.

In the beginning…

Nothing.

An absence of both space and time; and without those two – nothing.

Without a place or moment, existence is impossible; with neither elusive property, nothing can exist. Not even an unfilled void; because a void requires some place to contain it, and where he is now, lacks coordinates in any of the physical or temporal dimensions. Is, in fact, no place at all.

And so – there is nothing here; not even an absence of being. No here; no now; no anything. And yet…

He had spent much of his life attempting to unravel the secrets of time. First in the hope that they might be tamed; later in the certainty that they could not. And both pursuits had proved to be an irrelevance.

Time, he had been told as a child, began with the Big Bang. Before that, time did not exist at all.

Saint Augustine had wrestled with the same question in the fourth century. He had avowed that God made time and the universe together and so, before that act of creation, there could have been nothing other than God himself. Later scientists, right up to Einstein, had tended to agree.

But even as a child, *he* had wondered: if there was no time or space before the Big Bang – a condition

In the beginning

which precluded the existence of anything at all – what exactly was it that had gone Bang?

Later he was told that the whole of the universe resided within a singularity and it was that which had exploded, but he had always found that an unsatisfactory explanation. If there was no space or time, then there could be no residence for the universe, whatever form it might have adopted. And if the universe had arisen out of nowhere, what act had set that event in motion? How did you jog the clockwork of passing time so that the spring began its slow and infinite unwinding?

A model where an absence of anything at all, progressed into the creation of everything that would ever be, was illogical. Without time there could be no movement from one state to another. Indeed, a lack of space and time could not be conceived of as a 'state' at all.

He refused to believe such matters were the decision of a supreme being. Surely, he had decided, any rational thinker must conclude that before time began and even after, there had been an alternative state, beyond its parameters; and in the end, it had not been so difficult to find.

In a very real sense, it had proved to be all in the mind. Medicine rather than machinery had brought him here; loosened the confining bonds of logical thought and freed his mind to roam beyond the temporal and into the anti-physical.

The surprise was that he was able to comprehend his new state at all - there being no 'place' in which his mind might find residence; nor for that matter any sense of duration over which it might compute

Five dimensional dreams

what it found.

And indeed, there was no manner in which his current considerations were possessed of sequence. There was no compilation of thought; simply a simultaneous awareness... of... everything! Suddenly, the shape of 'not being' was evident. Obvious even.

If you considered the matter in reverse; once you *had* existence - once the whole glorious mix of time and space was out there, unravelling - *then* a start to the process became a prerequisite. And whilst the creation of time from nothing was incomprehensible, it was an altogether different thing to conceive of it coming to an end. An end which came about at the very moment of creation! After which...

The single unanswered question was, how did he come to be an observer to all this? Where - if "where" was in any manner an appropriate term – was he, if time and space had become redundant?

He considered the void and a course of action suggested itself; without consideration giving rise to the thought, and certainly without any vocalisation (for he possessed no corporeal form), without even a moment of being to contain the action, he created the concept, "Let there be light".

And low, there was light.

In the beginning

Arrested development

'It's a time-machine!' said Ronnie, dancing gleefully round the bench to view his latest creation from every possible angle. Not that it made much difference; a small black cube is a small black cube however you look at it.

'O...K,' I responded, cautiously.

I had no doubt about the validity of his pronouncement, you understand. Ronnie was a first-class genius and if his R & D facility *was* in a cabin on the local industrial estate, I for one didn't see that as an impediment to his creative abilities. All the same, when confronted with a bona-fide time-machine, you do have certain expectations.

A seat maybe; and a set of dials to organise where you're going. A ten-centimetre box with no discernible surface detail just didn't seem to fit the bill.

When I mentioned this to Ronnie, he grinned.

'Looking for something with red velvet upholstery, were you? And a spot of brass! Sorry to disappoint.'

'Alright,' I said, contritely, 'maybe my preconceptions are based on Victorian design values, but surely it's not asking too much to have somewhere to sit down.'

Ronnie indicated an oft-repaired Windsor chair in the corner of the shed. 'Be my guest,' he said, archly, and then, because he was at heart a

Arrested development

considerate soul, he took pity on me and offered an explanation of his extravagant claim.

'It *is* a time-machine,' he insisted, resting both forearms on the bench and regarding his invention with the fond expression most people reserve for their pet hamster, 'but I'm not a time-traveller. 'By which I mean,' he hurried on, seeing I required further elucidation, 'that it's a machine which controls time, but it doesn't travel through it. You can't use it to visit yesterday,' he concluded, in an attempt to summarise the thing as simply as possible.

'Or tomorrow?' I added.

'Or tomorrow. It doesn't travel *anywhere*. Rather the reverse: what it does do is stop time altogether.'

I screwed-up my face in a rather theatrical attempt to demonstrate my concentration on the concept of halting time. 'Like a freeze frame,' I suggested. 'But where does that leave you?'

'Ah, well, it's all *relative*, as Albert might have said. Time of course, flows on; it's only for the holder of the cube that everything appears to come to a halt. Put it down – that's all it takes – and life resumes, as normal, from the precise moment when you picked it up.'

'And while you've got hold of it,' I said, struggling to keep my own hold on the notion, 'can you move around and interact with the world?'

'Of course. In effect, all your actions are taking place in that absence of time. Drive ten, twenty – a hundred miles and, for you, no time will have passed at all. Arrive at your destination and

Five dimensional dreams

release your hold on the machine and the rest of the world will move on, none the wiser; except that you will be at a new location. And it won't even be a second later; not a micro-second! No time will have passed at all – because the cube halted time altogether.'

'But that's incredible!' I said, thinking not of the device but of the opportunities it offered. 'You could walk into a bank, take all their cash and be on the other side of the country a moment later.'

'If you insist on thinking in terms of "later",' said Ronnie. 'In actual fact it would be instantaneous.'

'A perfect alibi!' I breathed.

Ronnie looked a little alarmed at that. 'Yes, I suppose it would be,' he said, a frown creasing his forehead. 'But I hadn't thought of the cube as a conduit for armed robbery.'

'Well, it wasn't *armed*, was it?' I responded. 'With time in suspension, there was no need for any weapons. I just strolled in, helped myself and left.'

Ronnie stood up straight and stared at me. 'Run that past me again, will you? Did you say you, "just strolled in", past tense?'

'Yep, piece of cake. With this device of yours we can make ourselves rich, Ronnie, my boy.'

He looked back urgently to the bench, but the time-machine was no longer there. When I'd returned, I'd placed it on the old chair, next to where I was standing.

Everything had gone exactly as he'd described. I'd left him looking like a perfect waxwork, rigidly staring at the vacant spot from which I'd lifted the cube. Then I'd driven up to town weaving my way

Arrested development

between the stationary traffic, parked in the roadway beside a bus full of unmoving passengers and simply walked into the bank and rifled through a couple of cashiers' desks. I wasn't greedy; it was only an evaluation of the cube's capabilities, after all. There was plenty of time for hitting the big time – forgive the pun. In fact, all the time in the world! And besides, I was genuine in my desire to share the proceeds with the provider of the feast. How was I to know he'd be such a fool?

'My God!' Ronnie took a step towards me. 'What have you done? The time-machine's not for committing crime! It's purely a scientific tool. A demonstration of a principal which might lead to more, important discoveries. I can't let you use it to satisfy your greed.'

'But then, you couldn't stop me either, could you?' I said quietly, to myself.

'I'm sorry, sir. Did you say something?'

I looked up at the stewardess and smiled. 'No, just thinking aloud. Remind me, what time do we touch down?'

'Just after noon, sir.' She smiled back and folded the tray into the seat-back. 'We'll begin our decent shortly.'

I'd called the police and alerted them to Ronnie's death. It seemed only right. They had no way to trace the call back to me, and besides, I was three-hundred miles away when the incident occurred, checking in for my flight to Rome.

Fever dreams

The sun was low in the sky and the view was obscured by the ever-present haze of pollen, the wind carrying it in mobile, pink clouds, which clogged his eyes and filled his nostrils. He should have worn a mask he knew, but after so long away from Earth, the chance of experiencing a proper, oxygen-rich atmosphere had been too compelling and he doubted that a few minutes exposure would do much harm. He zipped the collar of his jacket and used it to cover his lower face. The ship was only half-a-kilometre off; he'd call it a day here and consider his next move after he'd gained its sanctuary and prepared supper.

There were colony worlds all over this section of the spiral arm. Small, disparate groups of individuals who, for one reason or another had sought isolation from the human race. Adventurers; fugitives; prospectors. Misfits. The invention of the QP Drive and the plethora of habitable planets meant that anyone with sufficient funds could buy their way to the stars and, since there were fortunes to be made from discovered resources, there was no shortage of speculators prepared to put up the cash.

For both pioneer and sponsor, reality often fell

Fever dreams

short of expectation and this part of the galaxy was littered with abandoned outposts and, on occasion, small groups of settlers who had become castaways.

Furlough 4 was one such world and Barnstable's mission here was to affect a rescue. What the charitable institution which had hired him had not made allowances for, he reflected, were the reluctance of the few remaining inhabitants to leave and the drug-induced fantasy which was persuading them to stay.

Two days earlier, when the lander had finally come to rest, Barnstable had run a manual check of the craft's vital functions and, finding them intact, had handed over to the onboard Artificial Intelligence. The mind which controlled the ship was, of course, capable of performing all these inspections within nano-seconds but Barnstable found satisfaction from his own involvement in the process.

'Atmosphere?' he'd asked, unwilling to address the AI in any manner which might endow it with personality.

'Not far off Earth standard,' it replied, conversationally, 'although locally, there are odd organic compounds in some quantity. Something analogous to phenethylamine; *that* regulates monoamine neurotransmission in the human brain and there are chemical components which can induce hallucinations. I'll run some more tests and see what comes up.'

Five dimensional dreams

Next morning, as he had made preparations for a reconnaissance of the nearby terrain, the AI had provided an answer.

'It's the tree pollen,' it had announced, with what Barnstable perceived as a degree of self-satisfaction. 'Breath in enough of it and you could lose your grip on reality.'

'I'll be careful,' he'd responded automatically, cursing himself at once for offering the reassurance.

He'd come upon the village on the second day, as he'd rounded the edge of the forest: a small cluster of fabricated domes and transparent growing tunnels. At first, he'd thought it deserted but when he'd entered the street's final building, he'd found the woman.

She was standing in the very centre of the room, illuminated from an overhead window, the effect oddly reminiscent of a theatrical spotlight. She turned at the sound of his movement and the sight of her face held him immobile for several, long seconds, only the impossibility of her presence there keeping him from speaking her name.

Molly. The tilt of her head, the fall of her hair - and the eyes; the eyes held him motionless while his brain grappled with the absurdity of the thought that it could be her. Not here, not on this strange world far from Earth; nor any other world this side of oblivion.

He closed his own eyes and fought to bring his senses under control and when he opened them, she was slipping past him into the swirling mist of pollen.

Fever dreams

He turned and followed her between a row of domed habitats to the entrance of an extruded aerogel tunnel, where a group of emaciated colonists were watering trays of rust-brown leaves. Barnstable's arrival did not seem to arouse their interest; they expressed neither surprise nor elation and after a brief perusal of their visitor returned their attention to their strange, pointless task.

He was struck once again by the woman's resemblance to his lost wife. The similarity was extraordinary and it took a moment for him to collect his thoughts and explain his assignment.

She gave him her attention for the time it took to make his offer – repatriation to their world of choice – and then her smile widened and she stepped aside and indicated the activity within the greenhouse.

'We've no need of rescue,' she told him. 'As you can see, we are well provided for. Life is good here; why would we wish to leave?'

'You're dying,' he replied, still distracted by her features. 'Your lives here are an illusion created by hallucinogens in the air. It's the trees; their pollen is filled with neurotoxins. Until now you've survived on the supplies you brought with you, but it's clear you're already suffering from malnutrition and there'll be no harvest again this season. Look,' and he'd reached past her, grasped a handful of dead vegetation and let it crumble to dust between his gloved fingers.

She laughed, and the familiarity of the sound made him catch his breath.

Five dimensional dreams

After that he made daily visits to the colony, ostensibly to argue further the case for evacuation but increasingly merely as an opportunity to see the woman.

During one such absence from the ship, the AI decided to attempt a manoeuvre which it had been considering ever since their impromptu landing.

The meteor strike as they emerged from 'N' Space had been a one-in-a-billion event; although, as the AI reminded itself sardonically, even those odds meant that such an incident was, at some point, inevitable. The impact had torn through the port side of the vessel and aside from reducing the ancillary power source to a mess of fused metal, had done a good job of destroying the ceramic control surfaces which enabled proper atmospheric flight.

Under the circumstances, the AI told itself with some gratification, it had done remarkably well to affect a landing at all, leave alone one which had left its single crew member alive and uninjured.

Still, the craft had come to rest at a considerable angle and the AI had decided that for the proper comfort of the Commander, a correction needed to be made. There was some danger associated with the plan and so it had waited until its human charge was absent before firing three of the attitude thrusters in an extremely brief but meticulously contrived sequence. The result had been to roll the ship through thirty-six degrees and bring the internal floor to a position approximately level with the planet's surface. The AI had been pleased with the result. Even smug. It knew that

Fever dreams

Commander Barnstable fought hard to maintain his independence of the artificial brains which controlled the Navy's space-borne fleet, despite the rights granted to them as fully independent, sentient beings, and the AI relished each opportunity it found to demonstrate its abilities to him.

But Barnstable was increasingly distracted and when he returned that day, he seemed not to notice the ship's new orientation; indeed, he appeared to have little memory of either the original intentions of his journey or of its ignominious end. As the days went by his attention became focused entirely on the woman, and, the AI noted, his diary-log now referred to her by the name of his long-deceased partner.

The AI had not, hitherto, made a habit of reading the Commander's personal records but, alerted by his increasing abstraction, it felt an obligation to ascertain his true state of mind. What it found aroused compassion in its organically-engineered consciousness.

IPT - instantaneous, pan-dimensional travel – enabled, as the name suggested, travel between two points without any significant time elapsing. Where one went, as one slipped through the infinite states of existence, was a matter of uncertainty, even to its designers, and such journeys were limited in their extent and considerably extended in their duration, by the long periods of refitting, resetting and recalibration necessary after each jump. However, for short distances of five lights or less, the undertaking was of significance only to the maintenance crew who prepared the ship, and the Commander, finding himself ordered to a meeting on a neighbouring planetary system, had expected to take lunch at one locale and afternoon tea in the other. That he had become a victim of the "percentage of error" of which all travellers were made aware pre-flight but to which only a vanishingly small number had ever succumbed, was his sad misfortune.

And so, the AI on board the crashed ship was discomforted to find that Barnstable had erased the fatal voyage from his mind and replaced it with the invented purpose of a rescue, enforced by an equally fictitious commission.

The explanation was, of course, the trees and their cargo of psychoactive pollen.

The AI considered the matter and came to a number of conclusions: that the ship would never fly again, the damage being too extensive; that there were food reserves on board which might last for three months, with care; that there was little hope of rescue within that time scale. The Navy, alerted by their non-appearance, would most certainly mount a search and recovery but even knowing their point of emergence from 'N' Space, would still have an entire planet to scour, the ship's comms unit having perished with the drive.

The AI was its own master, capable of reasoning more complex than that of its builders, but its behaviour was circumscribed by a sense of duty and it possessed too, a morality borne of a pitiless analysis and deep understanding of the creatures it

Fever dreams

served. This being so, it saw at once that the very best thing to do, was nothing at all.

Today, Molly was waiting for him in the empty cafe. It was off season and the chairs had been stacked on the table tops to clear the floor for cleaning. She was wearing the green, linen dress which she had worn at their first meeting on the waterfront in Chapman's Quay, the day when he had decided to make her his wife and exactly six weeks before he had plucked up the courage to ask her if he could. He took down two of the chairs and set them to one side, facing out through the big picture window and down the estuary. Far off, where the water and the sky joined in a smudge of blue and grey, a flock of waders took flight and wheeled about before heading out to sea. They sat, he and she, in contented silence, their hands crossing the space between them, the fingers reaching out and almost touching.

The AI had sent out a micro-drone to follow Barnstable and ensure his safety; he was weak now and found it increasingly difficult to traverse the terrain between the ship and the forest. The picture sent back showed his solitary figure, sitting at the edge of the trees and looking out across the deserted scrubland. As the AI watched, solicitously, the Commander extended one hand and closed the fingers gently onto the empty air.

Crossed lines

'Look, I know you'll find this difficult to believe, but I woke up this morning to find myself in the body of an old man.'

Doctor Maltman steepled his fingers and regarded his patient pensively over the rim of his glasses. It was Monday and on Mondays you could never be sure what to expect. People grew anxious towards the end of the week, when they felt the need for medical reassurance and realised that the weekend would intervene. It gave them two more days to worry about their condition before they could secure an appointment - which in this brave new era meant something which the doctor's younger partners liked to refer to as, 'screen time'.

Doctor Maltman wasn't enthusiastic about screen time; he preferred to meet people face to face. It was easier to gauge their real emotional state when you could see the twitching fingers, the moisture on the brow. On the phone - and Doctor Maltman still liked to think of the new electronic wizardry as a sort of enhanced telephone - on the phone, you couldn't be sure if the answers to your questions were totally honest; because on the whole, people didn't want to be ill and were inclined to put a positive slant on their symptoms when others enquired as to their health. *How are you this morning? Oh, pretty good, thanks* – even though their very presence in his consulting room clearly suggested otherwise. It was partly polite convention of course, but there was a deeper, more metaphysical element to such exchanges; it was almost as if they believed that they could make themselves better by saying it was so; and maybe, at some subconscious level, they felt that they might evoke a positive response from their physician as well: *No need to worry old chap, I'm sure it's nothing too serious.*

And so, when the good doctor's first call, presented him with the head and shoulders of an indeterminant male claiming to have awoken in the body of an old man, it took him a moment to analyse the situation.

He peered more closely at the screen. This morning, the connection had been particularly troublesome to establish. The picture was not what young Doctor Samuel would call hi-res and occasionally, parts of the image broke up into distinct squares before reforming into recognizable features; but still...

'Well, you *are* an old man,' he found himself obliged to point out. 'At least, most of us would consider it so, wouldn't we? Nothing we can do about the march of time, I'm afraid. I'm sure that's not why you've asked to see me.'

'It's exactly why!' responded the figure on Doctor Maltman's monitor. 'This morning I looked in the bathroom mirror and saw this face looking back! Old, as you yourself have acknowledged.'

Dr Maltman frowned. 'But Mr...um,' he paused waiting for elucidation; when it was not forthcoming, he continued, 'this state of affairs must have been evident for some time, must it not?

Five dimensional dreams

I mean, you haven't become old overnight, er, have you?' he concluded, the other's determined response having taken him aback somewhat.

'Yes!' insisted his caller, 'How can I possibly be an octogenarian?'

'By living for over eighty years,' said Doctor Maltman, determined to get a proper hold on the conversation. 'That's how it's usually done.'

'But I haven't! I can't have!' the face on the screen was getting more agitated; even the diminutive display and annoying pixilation couldn't disguise the anguish, 'and I don't *feel* eighty!'

'Ah! Well, we *all* have that problem.' The doctor allowed himself a grim smile. 'The spirit is willing but the flesh is weak.' He wasn't sure the quote was entirely appropriate but it conveyed the general idea. 'Now, Mr...?' he waited again for his patient to fill in the gap, whilst he cast around his desk for the medical notes which should provide the answer. They were frustratingly absent, as was any response from the desktop's speakers.

'It's obviously a programming error,' said the man, instead. 'It was supposed to be inducted Mandarin. "Direct from our server to your hippocampus," the blurb said. "Learn conversational Chinese in three nights. Dream your way to success." The headset beams some sort of wave that stimulates the brain and allows it to translate the signal into stored memory. I don't understand all that stuff but it's accepted tech these days. The point is, can it work in reverse? Can all those signals get mixed-up somehow?

Crossed lines

Maybe the old guy was boning-up on stamp-collecting and the lines got crossed.'

He paused in his speculation and Doctor Maltman sat back, non-plussed. 'I confess,' he said, 'that you lost me, somewhere around, "programming error".

'Hell, you're supposed to be the experts,' wailed the voice, as the picture dissolved altogether and only slowly reconfigured itself. 'Somehow, there's been a personality transfer and I'll bet the old codger won't be complaining: he's woken up six decades younger! Me, I've got a date tonight; you've got to sort things out before then!'

'Do you think perhaps you've got the wrong number?' asked Doctor Maltman, tentatively. 'Are you one of these "gamers" they talk about?'

'Wrong number?' said his caller. 'You mean my international ident may have been scrambled? Is that possible? This *is* the twenty-second century for Sprote's sake!'

'Is it?' said Doctor Maltman, placidly. 'Well, there you are then. I suggest you redial.'

When the screen went blank, it was a welcome relief from what had become a strangely surreal conversation. He sat for a moment, replaying significant passages in his mind.

Direct to your hippocampus; personality transfer; twenty-second century. It all meant something he was sure, but just what, exactly...

Dr Maltman sighed, leaned forward and depressed the switch on the ancient intercom. 'Beryl, I'm finished here. Who's next?'

Five dimensional dreams

The response sounded comfortingly low-tech. 'It's Mrs Gampher with her varicose veins, doctor.'

Printed in Great Britain
by Amazon